BOOK SEVEN VINCENT

T.O. SMITH

SAVAGE CROWS MC MOTHER CHARTER
BOOK SEVEN

T.O. SMITH					SCMC MOTHER CHARTER

For Riley, my reason for everything that I do.

For those of you who followed me to Amazon from Inkitt, you guys are absolutely amazing.

And for those of you who read the original Savage Crows MC series and decided to continue reading with the mother charter series, thank you!

©April 2022. T.O. Smith. All rights reserved.

No part of this book may be reproduced, distributed, or transmitted in any form or by any means, including photocopying, recording, or other electronic or mechanical systems, without written permission from the author, except for the use of brief quotations in a book review.

This book is a work of fiction. Names, characters, places, and incidents are either a product of the author's imagination or are used fictitiously, and any resemblance to actual persons, living or dead, events, or locales is entirely coincidental.

Cover Design: Tiff Writes Romance

Editing: Tiff Writes Romance

Proofreading: Kimberly Peterson, Taylor Jade

BOOKS IN THE SERIES

Brett - Book One

Kyle - Book Two

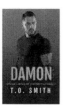
Damon - Book Three

Halen - Book Four

Logan - Book Five

Walker - Book Six

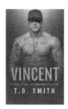
Vincent - Book Seven

SAVAGE CROWS MOTHER CHARTER

Copper - President
Damon - Vice President
Kyle - Road Captain
Halen - Sergeant at Arms
Vincent - Enforcer
Brett - Secretary
Logan - Treasurer
Walker - Chaplain

SAVAGE CROWS (TX CHARTER)

Blink: Founder
Grim: President
Alex: Vice President
Ink: Road Captain
Hatchet: Sergeant at Arms
Thor: Enforcer
Grave: Secretary
Bullet: Treasurer
Sabotage: Chaplain
Scab: Patch

SIDE NOTES

A chaplain is normally the one over all of the spiritual things in a club, as well as performs marriage ceremonies, funerals, and puts protection on members in jail.

A chaplain in my book is the one the members go to for advice. So, please keep that in mind while reading this book.

Thanks!

CHAPTER ONE
VINCENT

I stared after Walker as he marched up the stairs. Clearly, Nova leaving wasn't settling well with him. I didn't want him to do anything he wasn't ready for, but at the same time, I wasn't letting him drown in his fucking shit either.

We didn't work like that. We never had, and he had to know that I wasn't letting that shit start today.

I handed my beer off to Halen. He frowned at me. "Is he okay?"

I shook my head. "Probably fucking not," I muttered. "Get rid of that beer for me, yeah?"

I headed towards the stairs. When I walked into our apartment, Walker was sitting on the edge of the bed, the bottle tipped back as he guzzled the alcohol down his throat. I let loose a disgusted sound and locked the door behind me before marching over to him, snatching the bottle from his hand.

"What the fuck?!" he shouted at me as I walked over to the bathroom and poured the remainder of the liquid down the sink.

I swung around to face him, dropping the bottle into the trash can. "You want to let her walk away? Fine. Let her walk away. But don't wallow in a goddamn pity party either, you hear me? You're stronger than this shit, Walker."

He scoffed at me. "Do I *look* stronger than that, Vince?" he demanded. I hated the broken note seeping into his voice. Letting Nova walk away from him was fucking with his head and his heart. He wasn't going to hold himself together very well. "I'm not good for her, Vince. She deserves a second chance. She deserves something better than what you or I could give her. She deserves to just *live*, goddammit. We can't rip that from her by tying her down here as an old lady." His broken laugh ripped my fucking heart apart. "I mean, I'm barely holding myself together most days, Vince. I've got nothing to offer her but shattered pieces of myself. I don't even feel like a whole man anymore."

"Did you ever stop for one goddamn second to fucking consider if she *wants* all of your shattered pieces, Walker?" I demanded. I walked forward and knelt in front of him, grasping his face in my hands. "Baby, you are not worthless. Goddammit, I wish I could get that through your head. All your shattered pieces, I hold them in my hands every fucking day, and she just wants to be given the opportunity to do the same."

He swallowed thickly. "Then why didn't she stay?" he brokenly asked me. "Why didn't she make it clear that she wanted me?"

I brushed the pad of my thumb over his bottom lip. "She did," I said quietly. "But you're always so lost in your misery that you missed all the signs. She wasn't looking for an escape with you, Walker. She was looking for forever."

He swallowed thickly then shook his head. "I can't," he finally uttered. "This shit fucking hurts, but I won't do it to her."

I shook my head at him. "I will always tell you not to do anything until you're ready," I reminded him, "but don't let your fear keep you from something great."

Deciding to drop it, especially since I could sense him shutting down on me, I dragged his mouth down to mine and kissed him, intent on distracting him in the best way I knew how.

He moaned into my mouth, his hands pushing at my cut. I shrugged it off my shoulders before pulling my mouth from his to yank my shirt over my head. Then, I pressed a hand to his chest, gently pushing him back. "Lie down for me."

He did as I instructed, but not before he bared his glorious, upper body to me. Scars littered his chest and abdomen, racing down his arms, but he never looked better to me. Every time I feasted my eyes upon Walker, I felt even more blessed to fucking call him mine.

I just wish he could find that boldness and that fearlessness inside him that made him initiate our first kiss and what was possibly the hottest fucking night of my life.

I undid his belt buckle and unsnapped his jeans, tugging them down his legs. He kicked his boots off and let me drop his jeans completely. I pulled his briefs down next, his cock almost hitting me in the face. I grinned, finally getting what I was after.

I licked at his balls for a minute, relishing in the groans that tore from his throat. But finally, I wrapped my lips around the thick head of his cock, paying special attention to the tip as I lapped up the bead of precum on the tip.

Then, I swallowed him to the back of my throat. My palms were flattened on his thighs, holding his legs apart for me as I worshipped his dick with my tongue, not touching him with my hands.

Walker fucking loved it when I only used my mouth.

And just to tease him, I pretended to grab the base, backing off a little, and he growled, his fingers lacing in my hair as he began to fuck my mouth, taking what he wanted from me. He wasn't gentle; Walker never was, but I loved the brutal way he fucked.

Finally, his cum coated my tongue, and I greedily swallowed every drop before popping him out of my mouth. Then, I dropped my jeans, lubed up my cock, and sank into his ass. He stared up at me, his eyes not once leaving mine.

"You ready for this?" I asked him. I was about to give his mind the release it needed from the torment inside of it.

He nodded. "Give me your worst," he dared.

CHAPTER TWO

WALKER

I leaned my head down, letting my chin rest on my chest as the hot, scalding water rushed down my back. I'd woken up hungover as fuck this morning when my alarm went off. Though Kyle had told me I could take the day off to recuperate some more, I couldn't just sit around, not with my head the fucked-up mess that it was.

I couldn't get Nova out.

She was there—her fucking pretty smile, those large, trusting eyes. She was *everywhere*. It was just about suffocating me.

Vincent's hands slid up my back when he stepped into the shower. "You going to talk to me or just mope?" Vince asked.

I lifted my head and looked over my shoulder at him with a glare. God, he could be a dick sometimes, but I loved him for it. He always brought me out of my head.

"Not fucking moping, Vince."

He scoffed. "Like fuck you aren't, babe. You want her, you need to go after her. Otherwise, you need to pull your head out of your ass and move the fuck on. She thinks you don't want her." I sighed. "I can guarantee you that right now, she's looking for a rebound guy to lose herself in."

I gritted my teeth, my muscles bunching together, tension riding my shoulders. I couldn't stand the idea of her with another man, but I didn't fucking deserve her. It was selfish of me to ask her to be ours.

"Fuck off," I snarled at him.

Vince shrugged at me and dropped his hands. Silence rang through the bathroom as he quickly bathed and rinsed before getting out. I barely refrained from putting my fist through the bathroom wall.

Now, all I could picture was Nova fucking another man, moaning *his* name, begging for *his* cock.

Jesus Christ.

I quickly bathed and got out, needing to go lose myself in work as quickly as possible.

And try like hell to get Nova the fuck out of my head.

Work didn't do shit for me. In fact, I was pretty sure Vince was the only reason Kyle hadn't swung on me yet. Even

Copper was losing his patience with me. I was snapping at everybody, losing my fucking shit over the smallest things.

Vince understood. He knew I was on the edge of something dangerous, and I either needed to get myself down off that ledge, or I was going to fall.

And if I fell, God help us all.

Vince had talked me off the ledge once, but he knew this was something I had to do on my own. Because this wasn't something he could help me with anymore.

My demons were my own issues, and right now, they were crawling all over my skin and darkening my mind, affecting everyone around me.

"Alright, get out," Kyle barked at me. I looked up at him with a glare as I tossed down the wrench in my hand, not giving a fuck where it landed. "Skylar has just about had it with you throwing her fucking tools around, and my customers have had it with your nasty as fuck look when they walk in here. Go home, Walker. Come back when your head is back on straight."

I slammed the hood down on the car I'd been working on, itching for a fight. Vince quickly stepped between me and Kyle, preventing both of us from going at each other. Vince shot me a cold look. "Go, Walker. He's right. Your head isn't here. You need to sort that shit."

We stared at each other for a moment. It wasn't until his eyes softened that I backed down. Shaking my head, I thrust my greasy hands through my hair, looking up at Kyle. "I'm sorry, brother," I grunted. "Tell Skylar I'm sorry, too, yeah?"

He clapped a hand to my shoulder, no longer angry. It was how we worked. The men of this club would fight at the drop of a hat, but we were brothers before and after everything. "We all have dark shit to deal with, Walker. It's *how* we fucking deal with it that matters."

I nodded once and strode around him and Vincent, pulling my bike keys from my pocket. Copper nodded once at me. "Colors, brother."

I shot him a two fingers salute that would have pissed my drill sergeant off and gotten my ass smoked before I walked over to my bike. I shrugged my cut on before riding out, hoping a long drive would clear my head.

I caved thirty miles out of town.

I couldn't do it.

I couldn't let her go.

I got off my bike and turned towards the field beside me, staring out at all of the grass growing. It softly blew in the breeze, the sun making it seem so much greener. It was almost sunset, the sun low in the sky, reds and oranges already beginning to tinge the clouds.

"What?" Alejandro grumbled when he answered.

I sighed. I was probably about to get my ass chewed by him, but I'd take whatever he dished out. "How's Nova?" I asked him.

He grunted. "*Now* you want to know?"

I clenched my jaw. Looks like I couldn't fucking take it after all. "I didn't call to get the goddamn second degree from you, Alejandro. I want to know how she is."

"She's fucking miserable," he snapped down the line at me. "How the fuck do you expect her to be? Never seen her like this, Walker. What the fuck did you do to her?"

I swallowed thickly, my heart twisting in my chest. I'd never wanted to hurt her.

"I let her go," I whispered.

He sighed. "Men like you—like me—are not meant to be heroes, Walker. If we were, we certainly wouldn't be outlaws and criminals. So, stop trying to be a hero. Nova doesn't want that. She just wants *you*. So, I suggest you get your fucking head out of your ass and come get her. Her home is no longer here anymore. Her home is with *you*."

With that, he hung up, obviously done talking about it. With my heart racing in my chest, I called Vincent. I had to do this before I chickened out.

"Walker?" he asked.

I licked my lips. "I need you," I said quietly.

"Always here, babe," he reminded me. "So, talk." God, I loved this man.

I scrubbed my hand down my face. "I'm going to get Nova."

Vincent breathed a sigh of relief. "Glad you finally pulled your head out of your ass. I'll talk to Copper—get us a few days away from the club to get her and get her shit packed."

A small smile curved my lips. "Thanks for trying to knock some shit in my head."

He laughed softly. "I love you, Walker, but I'm not an enabler."

I grinned. No, he sure as fuck wasn't.

CHAPTER THREE
NOVA

I couldn't believe it had only been twenty-four hours since I'd walked away from Walker . . . and Vincent.

It felt like an eternity.

I'd cried a fuck ton. I had cried so much that my eyes were sore. My cheeks felt raw from swiping at them. And my poor nose was tender to the touch from blowing my nose so much.

Alejandro was torn between murdering Walker and ordering him to come get me. I'd told him to just leave it alone, that Walker would come to me when he was ready and not a moment sooner.

I wouldn't push a man that was suffering as much as Walker was to do something he wasn't ready for.

And he wasn't ready for everything that I had to offer him.

Because when it came down to it, I would give him every single piece of me. I would love him so much that he would feel overwhelmed at times.

And Vince . . . God. Who knew a man who normally seemed so hardened and brutal could love someone so much? His love for Walker spoke to me, and it made me love him for it. Someone who could love Walker as much as I did . . . there was no doubt in my mind that given the chance, Vince and I would form our own bond together.

I looked up at Alejandro as he stepped into the sitting room. I'd met Elaina earlier today, but she'd gone back home with Joey. I'd tried to get Alejandro to go, too, especially since he apparently spent most of his time in the states, but he refused, instead deciding to stay here with me.

It made me feel even worse that I was the reason he wasn't with his family.

"You look like shit," he noted.

I couldn't help it; I laughed, but it sounded as pathetic as I felt. "Feel like it, too," I confessed.

He sighed. "Is he worth all of this?" he asked, gesturing to the tissues in the trashcan next to me.

I just shrugged. "Yeah," I whispered. Alejandro just looked like he didn't understand one bit of it. "He's worth all of this and then some." I looked up at him. "You ever met someone and just . . . knew?"

Alejandro nodded. "I knew with Elaina, but our worlds were too fucked up to ever come together peacefully. She had to find her way to me."

I swallowed thickly and blew my nose again before speaking. "Then you understand why I can't force Walker to be with me."

He sighed. "Unfortunately, yes. I don't wish this pain on you, prima pequeña. You don't deserve it."

I smiled wryly. I'd missed someone talking to me in our native tongue. "I didn't deserve a lot of things that happened to me, Alejandro, but I deal. I live. I push through." Pain lanced through my chest. "And I'll survive this, too."

I would. I fucking had to. I hadn't come this far in my life to give up now, no matter how much it fucking hurt.

I pushed my eggs around on my plate, not hungry in the slightest. In fact, the thought of eating had my stomach turning.

I'd barely slept last night. Every time I closed my eyes, I saw Walker and Vince in my mind as if they were taunting me because I couldn't share with them what they had. I knew it wasn't real; I knew Vince would let me in if it was solely up to him, but it wasn't.

Walker had a say, too.

"Why aren't you eating?"

I jerked back in shock, my fork falling to my plate with a loud clatter. My eyes snapped up to see Walker and Vincent standing by the table, a frown on each of their faces. I opened and closed my mouth a few times, trying to figure out what the hell to say.

Was I happy to see both of them? Hell yes.

Was I also angry? A bit.

"Do you really want to know the answer to that?" I asked Walker, since he'd been the one to ask the question.

He crossed his arms over his chest, making his muscles bulge more than they already were. My core clenched. God, even angry and upset and fucking sad, I still wanted him. "Yeah, I do, actually."

I stood up from my seat and jabbed my finger against his chest. Every bit of hurt and pain I'd been feeling for the past thirty-something hours welled up inside of me, demanding release.

"Because *you* weren't man enough to face your shit and stop me from leaving."

He clenched his jaw and glanced over my head for a moment before he forced himself to relax. Surprising the fuck out of me, he cradled my jaw with his rough hands and leaned down, slanting his lips across mine in a kiss that had my fucking soul crying and my heart rejoicing.

This wasn't the kiss of a man that planned to tell me goodbye again.

This was the kiss of a man who had just finally come home.

"I'm sorry," he whispered, his lips rubbing mine. I clenched my eyes shut, tears welling up behind my closed lids. "I'm sorry I let you go. I'm never fucking doing it again." He leaned back up, his dark eyes meeting mine when I opened them. My breath left me on a shudder at the raw pain and sadness in his eyes. His demons were out to play, and I could see them wreaking havoc across his soul.

"Watching you leave with Alejandro was fucking brutal." He released me and scrubbed his hands down his face. I glanced over at Vincent. He was watching Walker, but when he felt his eyes on me, he glanced back at me, and a small smile tilted his lips in greeting that had my heart swelling in my chest. I looked back at Walker. "I want you like hell—want to keep you, Nova—but I don't have a goddamn thing to offer you."

I pressed my hands over his chest, taking a step closer to him as my heart bled for his. I just wanted to breathe life into him. "That's where you're wrong," I told him fiercely. "You may think you don't have anything to offer me, but this," I said, patting the spot right above his rapidly beating heart, "you can offer this."

He swallowed, staring down at me. "That easy?" he finally rasped.

I nodded. "That easy," I promised him. "With me, it will *always* be that easy."

He gathered me into his arms, crushing me against him. His strength and warmth wrapped around me, enveloping me in safety.

It took every bit of my restraint not to begin crying all over again. I really was so sick of crying all the time.

I felt Vincent's hand on my back. Walker slowly released me, and Vince turned me to face him. He tucked my hair behind my ear, his eyes boring into mine. "Will you come back with us, let us make this right with you?"

I smiled at him. "Is it temporary?"

Walker growled from behind me. "Fuck no."

I giggled, unable to help myself. These men really knew how to warm me up inside. "Then, yes, I'll come home with both of you."

Vince dropped a kiss to the top of my head before turning me back to Walker. He clapped Walker on the back. "I'm going to talk to Alejandro. You two make up, yeah?"

I watched as he walked off, his stride full of confidence. My body craved him just as much as it craved Walker, and I hadn't even been with Vincent yet.

Walker sighed softly, staring after him also. "You sure you're ready for both of us, baby girl?" he finally asked, looking back down at me.

I leaned up and pressed a kiss to the underside of his jaw. His eyes softened as they met mine. "If I can survive your mood swings," I teased, making him grin, "then I can survive being shared by two men."

He kissed me. "You're too fucking incredible to be true."

Vincent stepped outside. He was freshly showered, his shirt missing and only a pair of gray sweats riding low on his hips, revealing the imprint of his dick. My cheeks flushed, and I quickly looked away from him, staring back out over Alejandro's estate.

After dinner, he and Walker had used the gym in the house to work out, so I'd escaped outside with my favorite romance novel, slipping easily into the world of the characters.

"Good book?" he asked, taking a seat beside me.

I smiled. "One of my favorites," I informed him.

He dropped onto the swing beside me and draped an arm around my shoulders, tugging me closer to him. "You good?" he asked.

I looked up at him. "Honestly, yes." He dropped a kiss to my forehead. I sorely wanted to feel his lips on mine. He'd been refraining for so long; hell, we both had been. "I'm glad he finally came to his senses."

Vincent laughed softly. "It wasn't fucking easy," he told me. "The night you left, we had a bit of an argument. Fucker wanted to drink his sorrows away. I poured his alcohol down the drain."

I snorted. "Bet that went over well."

He grunted. "Yeah," he muttered. I could tell by his tone it had gone anything *but* well.

I glanced towards the back door. Walker was standing there, his arms crossed over his chest as he watched us. He inclined his head towards Vincent and winked at me. I blushed and leaned my head back on Vincent's shoulder.

"Pretty night," I said softly.

"Not as pretty as the image you make sitting beside me."

My cheeks warmed, and I glanced up at him. With a soft growl, Vince lowered his head to mine, his lips covering mine. I moaned into the kiss, our tongues dancing together. He gripped my waist and lifted me onto his lap, my knees settled on either side of him.

"*Fuck,*" Vincent rasped, his mouth moving down my neck, nipping at my skin. "You're goddamn *intoxicating.*"

I dragged his mouth back to mine just as Walker stepped outside. He leaned over the back of the swing, his lips at Vincent's ear. Vince groaned, thrusting up against my pussy. I cried out into our kiss.

"See how incredible she feels?" Walker whispered. "*Taste her, Vince.*"

So, Vince plundered my mouth and gave me the hottest make-out session I'd ever had in my life. The man was fucking skilled with his tongue.

CHAPTER FOUR
VINCENT

I rolled my head around on my shoulders, picking up my pace on the treadmill. It was six in the morning, but I was still stuck on military time—probably would be for the rest of my life. When I'd woken up, Nova was still passed out between me and Walker, and Walker was snoring lightly on the other side of her, finally getting some decent sleep.

So, I'd slipped out of bed as stealthily as I could since I didn't want to wake them, tugged on my sweats and a t-shirt, and came down to work out.

My head was filled with thoughts of Nova, much of the same way as it normally was with Walker. Now, they were crowded in my mind together, taking up every bit of available space.

I was honestly a bit astounded at how quickly I seemed to be getting attached to Nova. I'd wanted her for Walker. Him sharing her with me sometimes would have just been a positive because, I mean, who the fuck didn't love pussy?

But she was so much more than that.

The woman had gone through hell and back, had probably been sold more times than I could count on my fingers, and she still loved and cared so freely without ever asking for someone to love her in return.

If Walker hadn't finally made up his mind, she would have gone on with her life and slowly allowed herself to heal from the pain of losing him.

The woman was fucking incredible. Guys like me didn't deserve her. But Walker? He deserved her *and* needed her.

Alejandro stepped into the gym and leaned on the front of the treadmill I was using, dragging me out of my head. "Hate to send you on your way, but if you're taking Nova with you, I need you guys out by twelve. I need to head up to the Sons of Hells."

I pressed the cool down button, nodding at him. "I'll let Nova know so she can pack."

He slapped his hand to the top of the machine, nodded once, and disappeared back out of the gym. I smirked at his back.

The man liked to act like a hard ass, but if there was one person in this world who could soften him up, it was Elaina—Joey's old lady. Most people didn't even *try* to begin to understand what she and Alejandro had together. Because, for him, the cartel would always come first. But if someone fucked with her, Alejandro was the deadliest mother fucker you'd ever come across.

BOOK SEVEN   VINCENT

Walker was in the kitchen with Nova when I emerged back downstairs after a cool shower. She was eating breakfast, and he was drinking a cup of coffee.

"You coming back with us for sure?" I asked Nova. I pressed a kiss to Walker's lips when he handed me a cup of coffee.

"Yes. Why?" she asked, looking up at me from her plate.

My eyes dropped to her lips for a second, and my dick jumped in my jeans as I remembered kissing her, my tongue hot in her mouth as Walker whispered in my ear.

Fuck.

"Alejandro wants to go see Elaina," I told her. "We need to be out of here by twelve."

She nodded with a small shrug. "I don't have much to pack. It won't take me long."

I dropped a kiss to her head before sitting beside her. I looked up at Walker. "You feeling okay?"

He nodded. "No flashbacks," he quietly told me. "Slept like the fucking dead."

Thank fuck. He'd been goddamn miserable since he left to protect Nova. I grinned. "You needed that."

He grunted. "Fuck yeah, I did. I can't remember the last time I slept that long or that hard."

Nova smiled down at her plate. I slid my hand over her thigh, giving it a gentle squeeze.

It was because of her, and I had no doubt about that in my mind.

Copper was outside smoking when we pulled onto the lot. He watched as we parked our bikes, and Walker helped Nova off the back of his as much as he could without getting up. I walked up to Copper while Walker grabbed Nova's small duffel of things.

We really needed to take the woman shopping. She hadn't been kidding when she said she didn't have much. But that was to be expected considering when she'd been rescued, she'd just been shipped to the mountains.

"She here for good?" Copper asked me, nodding his head in the direction of Nova.

I nodded. He grunted. "Figured." He put out his cigarette. "Walker going to be able to handle that?"

I frowned at him, his comment rubbing me all the wrong fucking way. "Fuck is that supposed to mean, prez?"

He cast me a deadpan look. "I'm not stupid, Vincent. I notice everything. Don't know why you two are hiding it from the club, but that's your own shit to work out—not mine. But sometimes, he barely tolerates you when he gets in one of his moods. He'll chew a sweet woman like her up and spit her out."

I gritted my teeth but didn't say anything because I knew he was right. He stood and clapped a hand to my shoulder. "You'll keep him in line." He looked down at Nova as she walked up with Walker. "Welcome to the family, girly."

He gently squeezed her shoulder before heading inside. I smiled down at her. "Come on. Walker can drop your bag off upstairs in our apartment while I introduce you to everyone." I grabbed her hand in mine, nodding once at Walker. This was his opportunity to go take a breather, and I saw his shoulders relax.

Too much change bothered him. And though he'd wanted this, I knew he needed to take a moment to just breathe and remind himself everything was going to be okay.

Penny was the first one that walked up to us. "Nova?" she asked. Nova nodded a little awkwardly. "About damn time these two got a woman," she teased. She grabbed Nova's arm, pulling her away from me. "Come on. All of us ladies are in the kitchen putting together a big dinner. We could definitely use your help. I'm trying to start this once-a-week get-together thing . . ." her voice trailed off as they got farther away.

Halen snickered from behind me. "That got out of your hands fast."

I rolled my eyes. "She'll be fine." If there was one thing I knew about that woman, it was that she could hold her own. I dropped into a chair across from him. "Genesis in there, too?" I asked him.

He shook his head. "School, brother," he reminded me. "Not all of our women have set hours. She volunteered for some after-school thing that gives struggling students more one-on-one time. She'll be here in about," he looked at his watch, "two hours."

I shook my head. I didn't know how she managed two kids, her students, her damn wild ass husband, and then still took on more after school.

Skylar barged into the clubhouse. Kyle was behind her, laughing hard, their son on his hip. "Skylar, babe, come on. It's not that serious!" he called after her as she barged into the kitchen.

I arched an eyebrow at him as Walker came back downstairs. He dropped into the chair next to me, crossing his arms over his chest. Kyle dropped into the last chair at the table. "What happened?" Walker dared to ask.

Skylar was . . . wild. She didn't bite her tongue—not even with Copper. She was fierce, stood up for what she believed in, and took no shit.

She scared the hell out of most of us, to be honest.

"He decided that teaching our son a fucking nasty ass song about pussy was *appropriate*," Skylar snapped, coming back out of the kitchen with a beer in her hand.

"It was a *joke*," Kyle told her, still grinning.

She sneered at him. "Well, when his pre-k teacher calls and asks why he's rapping about pussy, you can tell her."

Walker grinned, laughing softly. "You fucked up, brother," Walker told him.

Skylar looked at us. "That new girl in there belong to you two?"

Walker rolled his eyes. "Yes," he told her. He then narrowed his eyes at her. "Don't fucking scare her."

Skylar snorted. "I think she and Penny were the only two that didn't scamper out of my way."

"Not true!" Cassidy called. "I just pick and choose my battles, that's all."

Skylar threw a smirk over her shoulder at her. Willow snorted. "Pick and choose your battles?" she asked. "Skylar will rip our heads from our shoulders."

I barked out a laugh at that one. Logan shot Skylar a dark look as he walked up behind her. "Watch yourself around my wife."

Skylar looked over her shoulder at him and scoffed. One thing you didn't do was fuck with Logan's wife, Willow. He was a force to be reckoned with about her. He was old enough to damn near be her dad, but the two of them worked fucking well together.

But he was *extremely* overprotective of her.

"You should let her defend herself," Skylar told him.

He dragged a chair over and straddled it, leaning his arms on the back of it. "She can, but that doesn't mean I'll ever make her."

Kyle arched an eyebrow at Logan. "How many times are you two going to have this discussion?"

"Not the first time?" I asked him. It was the first I was aware of it happening.

Kyle laughed and shook his head. "Nope. This shit happens at least once a week. Skylar is itching to get a reaction out of Willow, and she can't because Logan is always there."

Walker shrugged. "I'm on Logan's side." He looked up at Skylar. "But you can try with Nova. I won't interfere because I *know* she can stand her ground."

Speaking of Nova, she stepped out of the kitchen with two beers, walking over to us. She set mine down first and then handed Walker his. He grabbed her around the back of her thighs and pulled her closer. She leaned down and kissed him. I winked at her when he finally released her, her cheeks flushing.

"You fucking both of them?" Skylar bluntly asked her. I groaned. Leave it to fucking Skylar.

Jesus, she was in a mood.

Nova arched a brow at Skylar. "I am. That going to be a problem?"

Skylar shrugged. "Don't get favorites. Those two are like brothers to me. I won't take kindly to someone hurting them."

Nova smirked. "I'll be sure to make sure you can hear me screaming *both* of their names later so you can see firsthand that I don't do favorites."

With that, she strode off. I was shaking with laughter. Skylar was grinning.

"I fucking like her. You two chose well."

Walker smirked down into his beer.

CHAPTER FIVE
NOVA

Two days.

It had taken two days for Walker to withdraw from me.

We had been doing great. The three of us hadn't had sex yet, just enjoying being close to each other, exchanging *extremely* hot kisses, but it felt amazing. I loved every bit of just *being* with them.

But today, Walker's mind was elsewhere, and I could tell by the way he acted that he was pulling away from me.

He'd come after me. He had driven all the way to Mexico for me. I didn't understand why we were going through this yet again.

Vincent had already gone downstairs, leaving just me and Walker alone in the room. I wasn't sure if Vince could tell that something was wrong with Walker, but I certainly could. When I'd rolled over this morning to give him a kiss, he'd turned his head and got out of bed.

If that wasn't basically him waving a flag that screamed *something is wrong with me*, I didn't know what the hell was.

"Walker," I called when he stepped out of the bathroom in just a pair of jeans, all of his muscles on display, "can we talk?"

"About what?" he grunted, tugging a shirt over his head.

My hands trembled. I clasped them in my lap so he couldn't see. I didn't want him to see how badly this affected me. I didn't want him to push me away even further if he thought I couldn't handle his mood swings and the dark thoughts that clouded his mind.

Because I could. I could handle all of this. But that didn't mean that it didn't hurt.

"About this morning. You—"

"Nothing to talk about," he abruptly said, cutting me off.

I clenched my jaw and jumped off the bed, my ponytail swinging against my back. "Are you fucking kidding me right now?!" I exploded, all of my hurt welling up in my chest. His eyes snapped up to mine, surprise lighting up their depths. I clenched my jaw and stormed out of the room, afraid that if I stayed, I'd say something I regretted. And I didn't want to do that. Walker was fragile enough today, it seemed, and I didn't want to chance worsening that.

I slammed the room door on my way out. Vincent was already at the foot of the stairs when I came rushing down them.

"Fuck," he uttered, grabbing me in his arms as the first tear slid down my cheek. "Come on," he soothed, lifting me up.

I wound my arms and legs around him, burrowing my face in the curve of his neck as he walked outside, his hands holding the backs of my thighs. We settled onto the top of a picnic table, and Vince drew my face back, rubbing his thumbs over my wet cheeks.

"Talk to me," he coaxed.

My lips trembled. "Take me back home," I begged him.

He shook his head and wiped some tears from my cheeks. He didn't look the slightest bit alarmed by what I'd just said. He just remained calm and soothing. "Not happening, sweet girl. You can't run. That doesn't solve shit—usually just makes it worse. So tell me what happened."

I hiccupped. "Walker shut down on me this morning." Vincent quietly growled. I squeezed my eyes shut. "I tried to give him a kiss, and he turned away from me and got out of bed. I tried talking to him, but—" I hiccupped again, cutting myself off, "he told me there was nothing to talk about."

"Ah, babe," Vince crooned, pulling me back against his chest. I sobbed all while I inhaled his scent, trying to calm myself down. "I'll figure this out, darlin', but in the meantime, I don't want you going anywhere, you hear me?" He grabbed my face in his hands, resting his forehead on mine. Our eyes locked. "I want you here. We'll figure this shit out with Walker together, you hear me?"

My fingers trembled as I gripped his cut. "Was it always easy between you two?"

Vincent laughed and shook his head. "It took Walker a long time to come to terms with the fact that he wasn't the same guy that he was when we got together. He's got this idea in his head that he's just a bunch of shattered pieces." Vince shrugged. My heart felt like it was breaking at his words. "Fuck, baby girl, maybe he is. But I love each and every single one of those pieces. It took him a long time to believe that before he stopped pushing me away."

I licked my lips and sniffled. "Is it sad that I feel like he's worth all of this pain?"

Vincent shook his head. "It's not sad, baby girl. Because he *is* worth every bit of pain that he causes us. Because both of us know just how great of a guy there is beneath all his stone layers."

I swiped at my cheeks. We were quiet for a moment. Vincent just continued to hold me. "Sometimes, I don't feel like I'm enough for him," I confessed.

"Want to know something?" Vincent asked me. I looked up at him, my eyes blurry. "Sometimes, darlin', I don't feel like I'm enough for him either. But I keep pushing because I know Walker needs me. For me, that's my driving force. I can't ever give up on him because I love him so goddamn much and because I know without me, Walker would have given up a long time ago."

Sometimes, I found that hard to believe considering Walker and Vincent were so in tune with each other. I feared I would never have that with Walker. He was so hard to reach.

But fuck, I loved him, and I *couldn't* give up.

If I ran home right now to lick my wounds, that would destroy Walker.

Vincent smoothed his lips over mine. "Are you going to be okay while I go talk to him?"

Sniffling, I nodded and stood up from his lap. Vincent grabbed my hand and tugged me back between his legs. Cupping the back of my neck, he kissed me again, this kiss much deeper, his tongue dancing so erotically with mine that I was moaning, my hands clawing at him to bring him closer.

"Later," he promised me. He brushed the pad of his thumb over my bottom lip. "I've got to save our man before he self-destructs."

I watched as he jumped off the table and headed back inside the clubhouse. I blew out a soft breath and scrubbed my hands down my face.

I'm not giving up on you, Walker, no matter how much you may want me to.

CHAPTER SIX
VINCENT

This was not how I had wanted to start my Saturday. I'd had plans to surprise Nova and Walker with breakfast, but now, I had to go pull Walker's head out of his ass.

I had no doubt in my mind he'd probably had a nightmare or a flashback last night. I knew how badly they could set him back, how worthless it could make him feel.

But goddammit, he wasn't worthless. And if he didn't get his shit together and stop giving Nova the runaround, she was going to walk away from both of us. And I wouldn't stop her, no matter how much it might hurt me. Because I couldn't force her to keep suffering and getting hurt just because Walker couldn't get his own shit together.

Loving someone didn't mean you condoned all of their bullshit.

I pushed open the apartment door. Walker was sitting on the edge of the bed, his elbows braced on his knees, his hands dangling in front of him as he stared at the floor.

"What?" he growled.

I shut the door behind me. "Don't you fucking *what* me," I snapped at him. He drew his eyes from the floor to meet mine. "Nova is ready to walk," I gritted.

Fear of losing her flashed in his eyes. "Why?"

I wanted to smack him. "What the fuck do you mean *why*, Walker?" I barked. "Do you not remember how you fucking treated her this morning? She was in goddamn tears when she came to me!"

He flinched and scrubbed his hands down his face. "I had that same nightmare of her being killed last night," he confessed.

I sighed heavily, some of the fight dying out of me at his confession. "You think we can't protect her, babe?" I demanded to know. "Well, we damn well can't if you're pushing her away. Your constant back and forth is doing her head in. She doesn't deserve this shit while she's trying to heal, too. You seem to forget too damn easily that she's been through hell and back the past few years. The girl's survived and fought, but goddammit, she needs time to fucking *rest*. And you giving her this constant run around isn't helping her, Walker. It's fucking hindering her."

He swallowed thickly, but before he could answer, gunshots rang out. Walker and I both rushed for the door. "Nova!" he roared, his boots thundering down the steps, his gun already in his hand.

I covered him as he rushed outside. Copper and Damon were hiding to the sides of the door, trying to fire back. The other club members hadn't made it to the clubhouse yet for the day, and honestly, I was thankful.

Those women and kids didn't need to see this shit.

Nova's scream suddenly rang in my ears, chilling my bones.

"Fuck!" Walker roared, dropping by her side. He dropped his gun and grabbed her beneath her arms, dragging her back into the clubhouse while she screamed in agony. Once she was safely behind the clubhouse wall, I dropped my gun as well and ripped off my shirt and cut, pressing my shirt to her shoulder wound. It was pulsing blood. Her face was pale, screams of agony tearing from her lips.

"It hurts!" she screeched. She sobbed, tearing at my fucking heart as I navigated my phone with one hand, trying to call 9-1-1. "Help me, Walker," she cried.

"Breathe, baby," he tried soothing her as the gunshots died down, his words finally reaching my ears. "Breathe. Don't pass out, you hear me?"

I looked down at my soaked shirt, shaking my head. There was too much goddamn blood. "9-1-1, what's your emergency?"

"We need an ambulance." I rattled off the address to the clubhouse. "Victim is bleeding profusely from her shoulder. Might have nicked an artery. I'm applying pressure to the wound. No exit."

As soon as I received confirmation that help was on the way, I hung up the phone, tossing it onto my cut. Copper rushed over to us. "Penny is getting the kit."

I shook my head. "Help is on the way," I told him, watching as Walker cradled Nova's head in his lap. She was passing out, and Walker looked terrified. I'd never seen him so fucking scared in my life. I swallowed thickly. "Give me your shirt, Copper."

He ripped it off, handing it to me. I tossed my blood-soaked shirt aside and pressed the clean shirt to her wound. She moaned in pain, coming awake for just a moment before passing out again. I clenched my jaw.

"Copper, if she doesn't get help soon, we're going to lose her," I rasped.

He squeezed my shoulder, trying to help keep me grounded.

If I lost her, I'd burn the entire world to the ground in revenge.

CHAPTER SEVEN
NOVA

Completely passing out would have been a blessing, but I wasn't stupid. I knew I needed to stay awake, and I was struggling to.

I felt lethargic—weak. All I could focus on was the white-hot pain ripping through my shoulder. I felt like my head was going to explode.

It hurt so fucking bad!

I sobbed, and through the sound of my blood pounding in my ears, I could hear Walker trying to soothe me, but I couldn't make out his words. I could hear Vincent barking orders, but I didn't know what in the hell he was saying either.

I blinked my eyes slowly, Walker's hazy face coming into view. Darkness crept at the edges of my vision. I whimpered in pain, screaming again when something pressed against my shoulder.

Suddenly, people were surrounding me—people I didn't recognize. Walker moved, and I was lifted onto a stretcher. I couldn't keep my eyes open. I was so tired. I just wanted to sleep.

Loss of blood pulled me under, darkness wrapping me in its comforting, painless embrace.

Pain.

I moaned in discomfort, slowly opening my eyes to stare at the unfamiliar ceiling above me. The room I was in was mostly dark, just a small bit of light coming from behind an open door. The TV across from the bed I was on was turned to a news station.

Suddenly, a man's face filled my vision. Walker was staring down at me, concern and weariness swimming in the depths of his eyes. He looked tired.

"How are you feeling, baby?" he softly asked me, reaching out to rub his thumb over my cheek.

"Hurts," I mumbled, my eyes sliding closed for a second. God, why was I still so tired? I slowly opened my eyes again, staring back up at him. "How long was I out?"

"Few hours after your surgery," he told me. "Morphine has mostly kept you under."

I looked to my side when I heard someone move. Vincent's eyes met mine. He looked rough. Blood stained his jeans, and his cut was missing. I licked my dry lips. "Vince?" I questioned, the sound of my heart rate picking up on the monitor. Why did he have blood all over him? Was he hurt? "What—"

"Easy," he soothed, coming over to me. He grabbed my hand in his. "None of it is mine. It's all yours. You were bleeding a hell of a lot. You're goddamn lucky to be alive right now."

Walker's fingers curled around my jaw, and he turned my head so I was looking up at him again. "I'm sorry," he told me. My heart clenched in my chest. "I'm so goddamn sorry. I was terrified that I was losing you, and the last thing I'd done before you were shot was let you think I didn't want you." He shook his head. "I'll spend the rest of my life making that shit up to you."

I shook my head, feeling tired. I just wanted to sleep some more. "Don't. No regrets," I told him quietly. "I don't like them." I slowly opened my eyes back up. "Just stop pushing me away." I drew in a deep breath, moaning in pain when it strained my shoulder. "What happened? Why did I get shot?"

Vincent blew out a soft breath. "Someone ambushed the clubhouse. We don't know who. Copper and Alejandro are working together to figure out who the fuck it was."

"Texas Charter members are currently riding in," Walker told me. "It's going to be a full house for a while."

I frowned. I hated crowded places, but this was what I'd signed up for. I had decided to be with them, and that meant sometimes, I had to put up with their *very* large family.

"Cops?" I asked.

Vincent snorted, shaking his head at me. He gently squeezed my fingers. "You've got a lot to learn, sweet girl." He lifted my hand to his lips and pressed a kiss to the back of my fingers. "For now, I just want you to rest and get better so we can get you home. Let us worry about everything else."

I yawned again. "Will one of you lay with me?"

Vincent looked at Walker. "I need food and to check in with Copper. If you're good here with her—"

"I've got her," Walker assured him as he kicked off his boots.

Vincent pressed a kiss to my lips and brushed my hair behind my ear. "If you need me," he said, pressing a phone into my hand, "call me."

He kissed me one more time before he strode from the room, quietly shutting the door behind him. Walker eased me over onto the bed and laid down beside me. "I love you," he softly told me.

My heart swelled in my chest so much that it was slightly painful. I leaned my chin up and pressed my lips to his in a soft, slow kiss that seemed to mold our souls together.

"I've loved you from the moment you jumped out of that helicopter," I confessed.

He grinned. "Love at first sight?"

I smiled a little, though it probably looked a bit weird. The medication was pulling me back to sleep. "Something like that," I whispered. Though, in all honesty, it was because he had decided to put his life on the line to protect me. But I didn't have the energy anymore to force my lips to form those words.

He brushed his lips to the top of my head. "Sleep, baby girl."

So, I did. I slept wrapped up in my man's safe and comforting arms.

CHAPTER EIGHT
VINCENT

Copper was waiting outside for me when I rode onto the clubhouse lot. Blowing out a harsh breath, I killed my bike engine and pulled my helmet off my head.

"How is she?" he asked when I strode up to him.

"Awake. Good as she can be," I told him, which was the truth. I knew she was in pain despite the morphine drip they had her on. I glanced over at the spot she'd been shot at. It had been scrubbed clean, not a spot of blood anywhere.

And there had been so much goddamn blood.

It still made me sick to my stomach to know that it had come from her.

I knew as long as I looked at that spot for the rest of my life, I would see her bleeding out there.

"Walker is still with her?" Copper asked. I just nodded in answer. He clapped a hand to my shoulder. "We'll find who did this, Vince," he promised me.

We fucking better.

We walked inside the building. Ink, Thor, Bullet, and Grave were already seated at the table when I walked into the chapel. Ink was the road captain of the Texas charter; Thor was the enforcer, and Grave was the secretary. They nodded their heads in greeting to me, and I did the same before dropping into my seat, which happened to be next to Ink.

Ink was a ruthless son of a bitch, and he had a fucking nasty attitude to match it. But he was a good guy, definitely someone you wanted on your side.

"How's your woman?" he quietly asked me.

I just shrugged. "Good as she can be," I told him, repeating the same thing I'd said to Copper.

He grunted. Copper took a seat in his chair, bringing the table to order. "Word on the street is that a *very* old rival club is rebuilding. I'm talking about back when I first took the president patch kind of old." That was fucking *years* ago. Copper was in his fucking early twenties when he took the president patch, and the man was damn near mid-forty now.

"We need to shut them down *immediately*," he told us. "They're on our turf. And they had no morals back then, and I know they fucking won't now." He looked over at me. "You, Ink, Bullet, and Logan will go out for recon." Bullet was a patched member of the Texas charter. "I'll get the location to Walker of where Alejandro last knew they were at."

I nodded once. He pointed his finger at me. "No funny shit, Vincent. I know how fucking hot-headed you can be. You'll get your vengeance; it just won't be today." I clenched my jaw so tightly that my fucking molars hurt. "We're playing this safe and smart, you understand me? If we didn't have women and kids to worry about, then I'd say be my fucking guest, but too much rides on us being smart. Am I clear?"

"Fucking crystal," I snapped.

He narrowed his eyes at me for my attitude but nodded once and slammed his gavel on the table, adjourning church. I jerked to my feet, but a hand on my shoulder stopped me from storming out of the room. I slowly turned my head to face Ink.

"What?" I snapped.

He sighed. "I know how it feels, Vincent," he quietly told me. I grunted. "But Copper's right. Too much shit is riding on this. They already clipped your woman." I narrowed my eyes at him in warning to tread carefully before I lost my shit on him. "You want them to take out one of the other old ladies—fuck, one of the kids if you don't get them all?"

I knew he was right. I knew Copper was right.

Did that mean I had to like it?

Fuck no.

"Screw off, Ink," I growled. "I'm not fucking stupid. You don't know a single damn thing about me if you'd think I'd actually go off on my own like that."

With that, I spun on my heel. Ink gripped my arm again, swinging me back around to face him. "Not trying to start shit, brother, but sometimes we need to hear it bluntly put to us before we go do whatever the fuck we want to do anyway, regardless of the goddamn consequences."

I sighed and dropped back into my chair. Ink propped his hip against the table. The room had already cleared out, just leaving the two of us. I scrubbed my hands down my face. Sometimes, I felt like I could still see her blood all over my fucking skin.

"She almost bled out," I said quietly. "Nicked a fucking artery, Ink. She could have fucking *died*."

Ink took a seat in the chair beside me again. "Did anyone ever tell you what happened to Reina?" he quietly asked me.

I looked up at him. Reina was his old lady. He rarely ever talked about what happened between the two of them. I just knew she popped up at the clubhouse one day, caused a shit storm during a time of peace, and Ink had kept her as his old lady.

"I knew Reina in high school," he informed me. "Met her through Ghost. She's his little sister." I nodded because

I'd known that. It was common knowledge. Ghost was the road captain for the King's Disciples MC. "I loved her then, Vince, but she chose my older brother because he made moves before I did." He laughed softly. "I was worried about tainting her. She was sweet and kind, fucking brought color to this world, you know?"

I did know. It was how I'd felt about Walker, and it was now how I also felt about Nova.

"Jordan—my older brother—went to prison for a couple of years. Reina graduated high school. And he popped back up as if he'd never left her, blamed everything on me, and she fell right back into his trap." Ink shook his head. "Woman was a fucking glutton for punishment, I'd say. But she was also starved for love, and he was pretending to give it to her."

"So, she left," I said quietly.

He nodded. "Oh, she fucking left alright, but she didn't leave without making sure to tell me how much of a piece of shit I was." He snorted. My lips quirked with a smile. "Just for her to come running to me five years later because Jordan had been keeping her locked up in a cage like a fucking dog with numerous other women, raping them day in and day out."

Now that, I hadn't known. And it made me sick to my fucking stomach. Good thing the son of a bitch was dead.

"I wanted to destroy shit, Vince. I wanted to go after Jordan myself. Fuck, I even had it out with Sabotage when

I heard what she'd been going through. But I stayed with her until he came after her, and I had no choice. I went myself. Gave myself up to him." He looked up at me. "But you know what my heroics fucking got me, brother? They almost got me killed. Jordan beat the ever-living shit out of me. I almost didn't make it home to her. And that? Knowing I might have left her unprotected? That changed my outlook on shit a lot. It took me a little while, but it did."

I shook my head. "She would have had the club, brother."

Ink shrugged. "Maybe. Maybe even one of them would have taken her as their old lady." His face screwed up at that thought, making me snort. Ink was as possessive as they come. He looked at me. "But if something happened to you because you wanted to be rash, who's going to take care of Nova?"

"Walker," I said instantly. "We're both with her."

He leaned forward, carefully regarding me as he spoke his next words. "But let's say Walker is down for the count for whatever reason." He let me mull over that for a moment, and my gut twisted. "And she had no one." It was basically what happened on the mountains. I'd had to come to her rescue. Could I say one of the brothers would have? Not really. "Who'd take care of her then, Vincent?"

With that, he got up from his chair, leaving me to my thoughts.

Because he was right. While I was sure the club would take care of her, I didn't trust anyone but Walker to take care of her like I did. And if something happened to him?

Fuck.

Never had to worry about this kind of shit when I was just with a fucking man.

Looks like I was playing it safe.

Ink had known me too well. He knew if I let myself sit on it long enough, I'd do whatever the fuck I wanted anyway. Because he was like me—if we didn't take care of the shit ourselves, was there any real guarantee the problem would get fixed?

CHAPTER NINE
NOVA

After Vincent left, awkwardness settled in the room. Walker had hurt me; he knew that. I was trying to move past it; I just wanted to see him do something better, be the man I *knew* he could be. He just had to stop being so afraid first.

"I think I owe you an explanation," Walker quietly spoke up a little while later.

I looked over at him in silence, waiting on him to elaborate. He frowned down at his boots, for once looking unsure of himself. It wasn't a look that I liked seeing on him.

"Walker?" I softly asked, a bit worried now.

He cleared his throat before scrubbing his hand down his face. "My mom was strung out on drugs," he quietly began. "I was born prematurely—doctors didn't think I would survive that long," he confessed. "By a miracle, I pulled through."

My heart broke for him. Instantly, I knew that Walker's scars ran deep—too deep for maybe even me to touch and try to heal.

"I was in and out of the system a lot until I began learning how to hide the bruises." He leaned back in his chair. "Most kids might have enjoyed the reprieve, but not me. I couldn't stand all the constant changes. I need stability." He shrugged. "So, I hid the bruises and learned to keep my mouth shut."

"Oh, Walker," I whispered. My heart was crying for him. I wanted to wrap him up in my arms and hold him.

"Mom brought home men. Some of them—nah," he shook his head, "*most* of them—liked young boys, too." Tears burned in my eyes. I wanted to break his mother's neck and the neck of every man who ever touched his body without his permission. "I fought like hell, but most of the time, I wasn't successful."

My tears silently slid down my cheeks. I knew what it felt like to be raped, to be taken against my will, to have someone touching me that I hadn't allowed to.

My soul screamed for him, for the pain and scars I knew still lingered inside of him.

"I have nightmares," he told me, turning his head to finally look at me. His eyes looked haunted. "I have these nightmares that I can't save you." He swallowed thickly. "I can barely keep myself out of trouble, baby girl—can barely keep myself together these days. How the fuck am I expected to protect you and take care of you, too?"

I held my hand out, and he moved closer, lacing our fingers together before he pressed a gentle kiss to the back of my hand, right beneath my knuckles.

And right then, I knew I'd rather have a tiny bit of time with him than a lifetime without him.

I drew in a deep breath. "I'd rather live a short life by your side and have your love for that tiny bit of time than live a life without you, Walker." I drew in a ragged breath. "I love you—darkness and all. I'm not running away. I'm not leaving you. You, me, Vince—this thing isn't over between any of us until we're all lying dead in the ground," I swore.

He tightened his grip on my hand. Hope shone in his eyes, and in that hope, I could see the hope that maybe he wasn't so unworthy of my love after all. "You mean that?"

I nodded. "With every bit of my heart and soul," I swore.

With a rough exhale of relief, he stood, leaned over me, and slanted his lips across mine, giving me the softest, sweetest kiss I'd ever had in my life.

I pressed my finger to his lips once we parted. "But let me make myself clear on this note, Walker." His lips pulled into a frown immediately. "If you push me away again instead of talking to me, I'll walk. Nothing will stop me, and I won't turn back around. I'm worth more than that, and if you really, truly love me, you'll let me love you when you feel unworthy."

He clenched his jaw. "I don't deserve you, baby girl."

I shrugged. "That's your opinion. But I know you deserve a hell of a lot more than you let yourself believe."

With that, I pulled his face back down to mine.

CHAPTER TEN

VINCENT

I quietly stepped into the hospital room. It was well after visiting hours, but the staff pretended not to see me coming in through the emergency doors. It was one of the perks of being a member of the Savage Crows MC.

Walker was awake when I stepped in, but Nova was asleep, her chest slowly rising and falling, her lips softly parted. He stood and gripped the back of my neck, dragging my mouth to his. I softly groaned and gripped his hips, dragging him closer. He moaned softly into my mouth as our tongues danced together before we slowly parted.

"How is she?" I softly asked him, moving around him to go check on our girl.

"A bit weak still," he informed me. "They tried getting her to walk to the bathroom, but she almost passed out from dizziness. Blood loss is still fucking with her a bit."

I leaned down and softly brushed my lips across her cheek before I sat down on the long bench along the wall.

Walker sat beside me and grabbed my hand in his, lacing our fingers together.

"Found who's responsible," I quietly began. "Old crew from *years* ago—like back when Copper first got the president patch." Walker swore under his breath. "They're rebuilding from scratch. Seven of them where we scouted today. Seem to be a small group—didn't see anyone else come in, but doesn't necessarily mean there's not more."

"Then why aren't they already taken care of?" Walker quietly growled, obviously not pleased.

I gently squeezed his hand, trying to keep him calm. He blew out a harsh breath. "They're heavily fucking armed. Don't know what kind of shit we might be facing yet," I explained. And I knew we had to be smart about this. Ink and Copper had been right. We could go into this shit hot-headed. "And there's cameras every goddamn where. Logan's pretty sure there's some we can't see, and until we account for all of them, it's too risky."

Walker gritted his teeth but nodded his head in understanding. I gripped his chin and turned his head to face me. "Me and you—we'll get our revenge for this, babe. I promise you that. But we need to be smart about it. She needs us alive."

He looked at Nova, and his face softened.

"She and I . . . talked," Walker quietly began a moment later.

I arched an eyebrow at him. "What kind of talk?"

He swallowed thickly. "The kind that reveals my demons."

I dragged his face to mine and hungrily kissed him, so goddamn proud of him for finally opening up to her. He moaned softly, our tongues clashing together as we took from each other.

We were both raggedly breathing once we separated. "I'm fucking proud of you," I told him in a haggard whisper. "I know it wasn't easy for you, baby." I kissed him again. "Now, all you've got to do is let her love you just as much as I do."

He blew out a soft breath, looking back at her again. I tightened my hand around his in understanding.

"I'm not letting her get away again."

That was all I needed to hear to know that he would do what it took to keep her by his side, even if that meant every single one of his demons came out to play.

CHAPTER ELEVEN
NOVA

It took a few more days, but the doctor finally deemed me well enough to go home, and I was more than ready. I was tired of being in a sterile hospital room, laying on a bed that barely allowed enough room for one of the guys to lay with me.

I was ready to lay in bed, sandwiched between both of my men.

Vincent gently turned me to face him once I got out of the SUV. He tenderly cupped my face in his large, calloused hands. "I need to catch up with Copper and the rest of the club. Walker will take care of you."

I bit back a sigh and nodded my head. Club came first; I knew that, understood it even. But it didn't make it suck any less.

He pressed a tender kiss to my forehead and strode ahead of me and Walker into the clubhouse. Walker grabbed my hand in his. "He's trying to take care of you," Walker softly told me as he led me to the clubhouse doors. "Right now, taking care of you means that we eliminate whoever the fuck did this to you."

I gently squeezed his hand, my way of letting him know that I understood that. Vincent was a caretaker. It was how he operated, and I loved that about him. I knew that he would inevitably be the glue that held the three of us together. He had an instinctual need to take care of both me and Walker.

The clubhouse was suspiciously empty when we walked inside. I frowned up at Walker. "Where is everyone?"

"Dealing with club shit," he told me. "Probably left the old ladies and kids at home. It's a trying time right now."

"Oh." I hadn't thought of that. It would be kind of stupid to group everyone together; it made the entire club an easier target.

Walker led me upstairs to the apartment I now shared with him and Vincent. I watched as he quietly shut the door behind us, flipping the lock. I looked up at him, my lips softly parting as he shrugged his cut off.

"You look like you could use a hot soak," he told me. "Vincent said something about having bath stuff delivered for you this morning."

My chest warmed at Vincent's thoughtful gesture, and I wished he were here so I could wrap my arms around him and give him a hot, sensual kiss in thanks.

"A hot bath sounds amazing," I agreed. I slid off my flats and with Walker's help, I eased out of my clothes until I was standing naked in front of him. He pressed a tender kiss to the outer edge of my bandage.

"I fucking hate that we didn't protect you from this."

I reached up with my good hand and turned his head so he was looking at me. "All I care about is that you came for me, that you didn't turn your back on me."

He leaned down to softly kiss me. "I'd never truly turn my back on you, Nova."

I smiled at him. He led me into the bathroom, and after he turned the water on and poured in Epsom salt and lavender-scented bubble bath, he stepped in before reaching out and gripping my hips, holding me steady as I stepped into the tub with him.

I didn't know how long we soaked, but I eventually fell asleep in the warmth and safety of Walker's arms, his chest evenly rising and falling behind me. But we must have soaked for a while because when I woke up, I was in bed, naked, and Vincent was cuddling me from behind, one hand splayed over my chest, the other folded beneath my head, acting as a pillow.

"Hey," he rasped, his voice husky.

"Hey yourself," I whispered. I quietly yawned. "Where did Walker go?"

"Had to do some recon and catch up with Copper. He'll be gone for a little while." He nuzzled the back of my neck. "You smell fucking amazing."

I giggled. "Thank you for the bath stuff."

He tightened his arm around me and ground lightly against my ass. My breath hitched in my throat, and I released a low moan. He was rock hard. "Anything for you, sweet girl." He pressed a tender kiss to my shoulder.

I rolled over onto my back with a wince and turned my head to let my eyes meet his. "Will you make love to me?"

His eyes darkened, and he slid his hand a little lower, right above my core. Every part of my body tingled in anticipation. "You think you're up for that?"

I licked my lips. My body was singing for him, desperate to know what it would feel like to be joined with my other man.

"So long as you're gentle," I whispered.

His lips met mine in a soft kiss as his fingers found my clit. He circled the tight nub for a minute, his tongue sliding erotically against mine before he dipped two fingers inside of me, curling them just right. I whimpered against his mouth, my thighs falling further apart. He groaned.

"You're so fucking wet. You always this wet for Walker, baby girl?"

"Yes," I moaned. "Vince, please—"

With a hungry growl, he moved between my legs. His dick was so hard, it looked like it might be painful. He stroked it a couple of times, his eyes meeting mine. "You want my mouth or my dick, sweet girl?"

I needed him inside of me.

"Dick," I breathed.

He pushed my thighs further apart and then slowly eased inside of me inch by inch. He was a little bigger than Walker—had more girth, though their length seemed to be the same. I sucked in a sharp breath of air, my body stretching for him.

"*Fuck*, you're so tight," Vincent hissed, sinking fully inside of my cunt.

"I need—" I whimpered. Oh, God, I needed him.

He braced himself above me on his elbows and rocked in and out of me, barely jostling my body, but somehow, he seemed to hit that sweet spot inside of me over and over, his pelvic bone bumping my clit with each thrust.

"Look at me," he growled when I shut my eyes, my orgasm about to wash over me. I ripped my eyes open with a whimper. "Look at me when you cum. I want you to remember who the fuck is inside of you."

I cried out, my back arching, my breath panting out of me, but my eyes never left his as my pussy clutched at his cock.

He shouted my name, coming inside of me, my walls milking his cock for everything he had to offer.

Vincent was cuddling me on the bed, both of us watching an action movie on TV when Walker strode into the room. He flashed me a wicked grin. There was some dirt smeared on his cheeks and forehead, and his cut and jeans were dusty.

"Smells like sex in here."

My cheeks warmed. "We, um . . ."

Walker strode towards me—still fully clothed—and gently rolled me onto my back before pulling me to the edge of the bed. "You clean her up?" he asked, his eyes not leaving my naked body. I flushed under his gaze, the anticipation of Walker's touch making my body erupt in goosebumps.

"Not yet. Been too lazy," Vincent drawled, his eyes hungry as he watched Walker kneel between my legs.

"Good. I want to taste you and her combined."

With that, he buried his face between my thighs, lapping at my pussy like he hadn't eaten in *days*. Vincent leaned down and kissed me, his palms kneading my breasts. I whimpered into his mouth, my body already coiling tight for release.

I cried out Walker's name as I came, and once he worked every drop from me that he could, he leaned over me, bracing his hands on either side of my head. I moaned when he licked his lips, a smirk on his lips. "Tastes like fucking Heaven," he rasped.

Then, right over my head, he grabbed the back of Vincent's neck and molded their lips together. And it had me wet and ready to go all over again.

CHAPTER TWELVE
VINCENT

Almost losing Nova must have put a fuck ton of shit into perspective for him because he was doing a hell of a lot better with her around. He seemed to have come to terms with the fact that she was here to stay. And while I knew he was the one who wanted her to come back, had told me he wanted to go get her, I wasn't sure he completely understood at the time what that meant.

But now?

His head was in this one hundred percent, and our woman was glowing with the attention we lavished upon her. And Walker was smiling a bit more, joking a bit more—just being an all-around more pleasant guy to be around.

I was really fucking happy for it. Those two could relate to each other and touch each other's souls in a way I never would be able to. And I was okay with that.

I just wanted to see my man and woman fucking happy.

"Church in five," Copper suddenly barked as he came up the hallway, pulling his phone down from his ear.

Fuck, that didn't sound good.

Walker and I both got up from where we were sitting with Nova. I dropped a kiss to the top of her head. "Hang with one of the old ladies, yeah?" With that, I strode towards the chapel, feeling her worried gaze on my back.

Today was supposed to be a day to chill and allow Nova to really get to know everyone. But if club business called, we moved.

Once we were all seated at the table and the chapel doors were closed, Copper began church. "Got some intel," he told us. "Logan called me. I've been having him look into everything for us."

Of course, he had. And I had a feeling Logan would have done it with or without the president's orders. He had tools at his disposal that we didn't. Logan normally tried to keep his security firm and the club separate, but more and more lately, that line between the two had been getting blurred.

"He has the location of all cameras and has hacked into their system. If we're moving, we need to move now while no one knows he's in their shit." I nodded in agreement. Walker grunted next to me. "I want a pair on each side of the compound, and I want to surprise their asses with gunfire just like they fucking did us. The president comes back here alive," he ordered. "I want him in my mother fucking basement."

"The rest?" Halen asked, leaning back in his chair, looking a bit too excited for this shit.

The man was unhinged sometimes.

"Kill them all," Copper snarled. "I don't want a man left breathing except for that fucking president. Do I make myself clear?"

We all gave our affirmatives. "Three men stay behind and do clean up. Logan is making sure police aren't notified of this shit." Logan was a fucking tech whiz, hence why his security business did so goddamn well. "Get the scene cleaned up—nothing gets left behind to show we did this, clear?"

We all gave our affirmatives again. He nodded once, and we began discussing strategy.

I was ready to kill the mother fuckers for what the fuck happened to Nova, and with one look at Walker, I could tell by the dark, glittering look in his eyes that he was more than fucking ready for this, too.

Bring on the fucking bloodshed. I was ready to coat my hands red.

I made a motion to Walker, letting him know I was walking in. He nodded once, motioning that he had my back, and we slipped through the gate. We didn't have any colors on, our club cuts back at the clubhouse in the apartment upstairs. Every single member was wearing all black with masks over our faces so we couldn't be identified.

I popped off two shots, sinking a bullet in each man's head as they turned towards us. The gravel lot didn't help matters much since the rocks moved beneath our boots, but Walker and I knew how to navigate this shit, and we worked well together.

We always had. Our military training had never left us, and it was like second nature to navigate a terrain like this. Hell, this was one of the easiest things we'd done.

Finally, the sound I needed to hear met my ears. A shout rang out, and then it was fucking chaos from there. Walker and I marched through the compound, dodging bullets as we hunted down the president.

Walker made a motion to me as we plastered ourselves against a wall so bullets couldn't hit us. He pointed up ahead where someone had just poked his head around a corner. I grinned, and we dropped low to the floor, moving as fast as we could in a squat to get to the fucker who was in hiding.

"Surprise, mother fucker," I breathed as I stood to my feet, pressing the barrel of my gun to the back of his neck when I crept up behind him.

He quickly dropped his gun and put his hands up. Walker moved around me, a malicious grin pulling at his lips.

"Surprise indeed," Walker agreed. With that, he slammed the butt of his gun into the asshole's abdomen, a snarl twisting his lips. "That's for almost killing my woman." He looked up at me. "Let's get him the fuck out of here."

Unable to help myself, I gripped the back of Walker's neck and pressed my lips to his. "Fucking love it when you get pissed like that."

He just grinned at me.

CHAPTER THIRTEEN
VINCENT

Walker and I jumped out of the SUV at the same time. Halen followed out right behind us. I looked at Walker. "Get Nova upstairs," I ordered. "She doesn't need to see this shit."

He nodded once and headed inside. Halen and I grabbed the president out of the back. He was already awake, and he was putting up a hell of a fight, trying to wiggle his way out of our grip. Halen grunted and suddenly stopped. "If you don't stop moving," Halen snarled into the man's angry, red face, "I'll fucking kill you my goddamn self."

The president tried to say something, but it was muffled by the gag in his mouth. Together, we managed to get him into the clubhouse and down into the basement. Halen and I dropped him to the cement floor, and he groaned in pain, rolling to his side.

Copper stepped down the stairs, his eyes on the president. "Well, well, well. Thought I was done with you sons of bitches years ago." He looked at me. "Remove the gag."

I did as he ordered, tossing the bandana down on the floor before stepping back. Copper grabbed a bat off the wall. "You look just like your dad, kid."

The man just sneered at him. I stayed silent, standing beside Halen as we watched the scene in front of us unfold. Copper tapped the bat against his thigh. "Johnson managed to keep your existence under tight wraps, even after death," Copper mused. "Tell me, kid; what the fuck did you think was going to happen when you shot up my warehouse, almost killed one of the women?"

The man just gritted his teeth, refusing to answer. Copper shrugged. "Makes no difference to me if you answer my questions or not."

With that, Copper swung the bat down, and the first scream of many echoed in the basement.

After watching Copper beat the asshole until he was unrecognizable and then marking him afterward, I had too much pent-up energy inside of me. Seeing that shit had me itching to do the same, but he was the only one we'd kept alive.

Nova looked up as I came into the room. Her eyes ran over me.

And somehow, she knew.

Without a word, she stood from the bed and pulled the large shirt she was wearing over her head. I growled softly, my hands clenching into fists at my sides. Her tits were large and heavy, begging for me to touch them.

She hooked her thumbs in her panties and slowly slid them down, her gaze never wavering from mine.

"I'm not afraid of you, Vincent." A coy smile tilted her lips. "Do your worst."

I glanced at Walker. He knew how I could get. He knew the roughness of my touch when I felt volatile.

He nodded once at me. That was all the signal I needed to know that she could handle whatever I dished out.

I gripped her hair and spun her around to face the bed. Walker grabbed her hands and anchored them to the bed at her sides as I yanked her hips back, forcing her into a perfect, ninety-degree angle.

And then, I was inside of her. She was already wet for me. I moaned at the feel and leaned over her, gripping her tits in my hands. I pulled at her tight nipples as I pounded into her, fucking her hard and fast. She whimpered my name, her breaths coming in short, quick pants as I wreaked havoc on her sweet cunt.

Walker continued keeping her pinned, but with his other hand, he pulled his dick out of his jeans and began to stroke himself, his pupils just about fucking blown as he watched me fuck our woman.

And that sent me toppling over the edge of sanity.

I gripped her hips so tightly I knew I'd bruise her flesh, and I fucked her until she had tears running down her face.

But even then, she just pleaded for more.

And I gave it to her.

Walker finally released her, and she clenched her fists, staying in position. "What are you—ah, fuck," I hissed when Walker moved behind me, pushing me forward a little bit.

I continued punishing Nova's sweet cunt as Walker rubbed lube into my ass. And then, he sank into me. I couldn't help the gasp that ripped from my lips, and then I moaned—long and loud—as Walker began to fuck me the same way I was fucking Nova.

I roared as I came, my vision momentarily going black. The only thing that kept me from crushing Nova was Walker's arm wrapped around me, his hand splayed over my chest, right above my rapidly beating heart.

"Move, baby girl," Walker rasped from behind me.

With a whimper, Nova moved from beneath me. Walker sucked lightly at my earlobe as Nova's large eyes locked on mine, nothing but lust and love for us in her gaze as she watched our man fuck me.

"Eat her out. She deserves it after the way you just fucked her," Walker rasped in my ear.

I sure as fuck didn't have to be told twice. I dragged her thick thighs apart and speared her with my tongue all while Walker punished me from behind.

Nova was dead on her feet by the time Walker and I were done. She was still trembling as we bathed her in the shower. And she ended up passing out as we waited on Walker to finish bathing so we could dry her off and put her to bed.

Our poor woman didn't even stir as we maneuvered her and dried her off. She was snoring, her lips softly parted.

It was honestly fucking adorable.

Walker leaned over Nova, who was sandwiched between our bodies, and kissed me. "Sometimes, I think I should be worried about how turned on you get when you see violent shit," he smirked, "but then again, we'd be missing out on some hot as fuck sex."

I ran my hand over the curve in Nova's waist. "You think she handled it okay?"

Walker snorted. "Babe, if she wasn't on the verge of passing out, I'm pretty sure she would have still been begging for more."

I tightened my arm around her. We'd gotten lucky as fuck meeting Nova, and I'd been lucky enough for Walker to want her to be a part of our lives.

She meant the entire fucking world to me—had come to mean so much to me in such a short amount of time. I never wanted to let her go. I'd fight like hell to keep her with me.

Not many women could handle the kind of monster I could turn into. But Nova? I could tell she craved the monster that resided within me.

And that touched me in a way only Walker had ever been capable of doing.

She was stuck with us for eternity, and I hoped she was damn ready for that.

CHAPTER FOURTEEN
NOVA

Being with both men had been . . . incredible, to say the least.

They were both so attentive and loving in their own ways. The kind of love I didn't receive from one, the other more than made up for it. Walker and Vincent were so different and had totally different love languages, but they evened each other out. I never felt overwhelmed when I was with both of them.

Instead, every single day—day in and day out—I felt loved, cared for, and taken care of.

And while I figured maybe someone would have something to say, everyone had welcomed me in with open arms. Even Skylar had, and she was tough as nails. Penny was always very sweet and motherly. At first, I'd truly wondered how she and Copper had ended up together, but seeing the two of them interact—it made sense.

Cassidy was quiet but sweet, always making sure I was comfortable. She was motherly in her own way, but not as much as Penny was.

And then Genesis. I hadn't known what to make of her at first, but the moment she opened her mouth, I knew instantly why Halen fell for her. She was full of sweet spark and tender fire. And between her and Skylar, I always had a smile on my face around them.

And then, there was Willow—sweet, quiet Willow. Her name said it all. She was the sort of person you just found comfort in being around. And while she and Logan had a lot of years separating them, I had yet to see any two people so openly devoted to each other.

This club—it was family. They may not be blood-related, but they were family all the same. Each and every single one of them came from something screwed up and found comfort in being around other souls like theirs. And together, all their fractured pieces came together to form something so beautiful and envious.

And now, I was a part of that.

Penny smacked my hand when I reached forward for the umpteenth time to help make breakfast. "Skylar, get her ass in a chair. She needs to rest."

Skylar grinned at me. "The mother bear has spoken. Find a seat." Penny cut her a dark look at that, but Skylar simply chose to ignore her.

I huffed. "I just want to help. My shoulder is injured, but I still have a good arm."

"And we don't care," Genesis retorted. "We want you to sit. So, sit."

I plopped my ass onto a bar stool with a scowl. Willow smiled at me. "Trust me, you're better off listening when those three order you to do something."

I just plopped my chin into my hand. Cassidy set a cup of coffee in front of me. "You look like you could use this."

I sighed and lifted the mug to my lips. "Thanks," I told her, meaning it. I hadn't had coffee yet this morning, but when I'd come downstairs and found them all in the kitchen making a big breakfast, I'd wanted to help.

Penny wasn't having any of it though. You'd think I was crippled with two broken legs and two broken arms with the way she was treating me.

The kitchen door swung open, and I turned to see one of my men stride in, though he halted at the sight of all the women. Hell, the only one missing was Olivia. Penny smiled at Vince. "Take your woman out of here before I beat her with a wooden spoon to make her listen."

I shot her a deadpan look. "I might like it," I retorted.

That brought a round of laughter in the kitchen. Vincent grinned at me and dropped a kiss to my lips. "Come on, baby girl. If Penny orders you to do something, you do it."

Sighing, I stepped down from the barstool. Penny smiled at me. "Not that we don't appreciate your help, Nova, because we do. We just want you to heal and get better first."

I offered her a smile in return. "I know. I just hate feeling like an invalid."

She scoffed. "The way Olivia said she heard you screaming last night—"

I cut her off. "Okay!" I said loudly, making everyone laugh. "That's enough. Where is Olivia anyway?"

"Trying to catch up on sleep, probably," Skylar teased, making my olive skin flush.

I rolled my eyes and stepped out of the kitchen, my cheeks warm. Vincent was softly laughing as he led me over to a table where Walker and Brett were sitting. Walker tugged me down onto his lap as soon as I reached him, and he leaned down, slanting his lips across mine.

"Didn't get enough of her last night?" Brett teased, bringing his mug of coffee to his lips.

I scowled at him. "Not you, too," I grumbled.

He laughed quietly. I rested my head on Walker's shoulder as Vincent grabbed my legs and draped them across his lap.

This was another thing about them. How they felt about me was in their actions. I'd never been loved or taken care of like this before in my life, and yet, they did it so effortlessly.

Feeling my eyes on him as he was talking to Brett, Vincent suddenly looked over at me. Without a word, he slid his hand over my thigh, giving it a gentle squeeze before he looked back at Brett.

I smiled—couldn't help myself. I really did love these men on a level I didn't think was possible.

I arched a brow at my cousin as he stepped into the clubhouse. Two of his men flanked him like they normally did. He nodded once at Walker and Brett before looking at me. "I need you to come with me."

"What the fuck for?" Walker demanded, sitting up straighter.

Alejandro looked at him, narrowing his eyes. I rested my hand on Walker's shoulder. "It's a family matter. I'd rather talk to her on her own about it first."

I grabbed Walker's hand and gave it a gentle squeeze. "He's my cousin. He won't let anything happen to me," I assured him.

He sighed and leaned over, pressing a hot kiss to my lips. "I'll let Vince know what's going on."

I stood from my chair and pulled my phone out of my pocket, shooting Vincent a quick text anyway as I followed Alejandro out of the clubhouse.

Alejandro needs to talk to me about something. I'll be back later. -Nova

His response was almost immediate, and it made me smile.

Keep your location on. I love you. -Vincent

Alejandro ended up taking me to some fancy restaurant a couple of towns over. I was definitely underdressed in just a pair of jeans and a baggy t-shirt, but no one batted an eye.

Alejandro had that kind of effect on people.

Once we were seated and Alejandro had ordered a bottle of wine, he gave me his undivided attention. "I've already put in our orders for the evening. I want this conversation to be disrupted as little as possible," he told me as the waiter came back. He simply set the bottle of wine down on the table and moved away, quickly giving us privacy again.

"Alejandro, you're beginning to worry me," I confessed. He was acting abnormally.

He sighed and reached into his jacket pocket, handing me a thick envelope. I slid the folded papers out. It was paperwork on a bank account.

Frowning, I looked back up at him. Why was he giving me bank account information?

"I don't understand."

"Your parents died at a young age," he told me. I nodded; I knew that already. Alejandro had rescued me the night they died so I wouldn't become a murder victim, too. "Their death was brutal and unexpected. *Padre* did not put enough protection on your family. He paid the price for that."

I didn't need to hear him say it to know that he'd been the one to make his father pay that price. Alejandro had loved my parents deeply. They were more of parents to him than his own father had been.

"They left you a hefty inheritance," he explained. My eyes widened in disbelief. "You have five accounts in your name; they did not want all of it in one place. But they have stipulations—don't want you to have it all at once. You should have received the first when you were eighteen. You'll receive the next one on your birthday."

I swallowed thickly, staring down at the papers in front of me. "How much?" I asked him quietly.

He paused while the waiter brought our food to us. Alejandro nodded once at him, and the young boy walked away again without another word.

"That account holds one million," he informed me. I sucked in a sharp breath of air. *That was quite a bit.* "That barely scrapes the surface of what you've been left. Your next inheritance will be a bit more, and so on and so forth."

I'd never realized my parents had been so wealthy. They'd always raised me humbly. We lived in a simple two-story house on a small plot of land. They hadn't ever wanted much, and they never bought much.

"How . . ."

"They wanted you to have everything you could ever dream of, Nova. They wanted you to be able to branch away from our family and go on to do better, safer things." His lips quirked with the beginnings of a smile. "They're probably rolling over in their graves to see you with two motorcycle club members."

I laughed softly. Alejandro reached over and gently circled his hand around my wrist, giving it a light squeeze. "But they would be happy for you, Nova. Because despite the organization Walker and Vincent belong to, they love you. And they'll take care of you."

I looked up at him, tears swimming in my eyes. "You really think so? Even though I got shot?"

He nodded. "Even through all of that, Nova. Because honestly, it could have happened with or without you being part of the SCMC. People are caught in crossfires daily. At least your men knew how to keep you alive."

I licked my dry lips as a tear ran down my cheek. "And are you proud of me?"

Alejandro had been the closest thing I'd had to a parent growing up. I craved his approval.

Alejandro allowed himself to smile, which was a rare sight. "I'm incredibly proud of you, Nova. You went through hell and back, and you still continue to see all the colors of the world. I could never ask more from you than that."

I sniffled, my tears blurring my vision. "Thank you for saving me," I whispered.

He wrapped his fingers around mine. "I never stopped looking for you," he promised me.

CHAPTER FIFTEEN
NOVA

The ride back to the clubhouse was quiet—peaceful. And it gave me time to think about what I was going to do with this portion of my inheritance.

And it came to me the moment I laid eyes on Walker.

I wanted to open a shelter for other women like me—women on the run from abusive family members, boyfriends, women who were victims of sex trafficking and needed a safe place.

And I wanted the club's backing for protection. I wanted these women to feel safe in my facility while they recovered, regrouped, and got their lives back together.

"You look like you have something on your mind," Walker said as I walked up to where he was sitting, still in the same chair he'd been in when I'd left to go eat dinner with Alejandro.

"Is Vince still at the garage?" I asked him.

Frowning, Walker nodded. "Want me to tell him to get his ass to the clubhouse?"

I nodded. He grabbed my hand and pressed a kiss to my palm. "Go on up to the apartment. I'll get in touch with Vince."

"Thanks," I whispered.

I headed up the stairs, and once I was in our room, I set the thick envelope on the nightstand before dropping down onto the bed. I knew what I wanted, but if I couldn't get the club's backing, then that meant I had to get Alejandro's, which meant he'd have to permanently station men here. And I felt like that would be stepping on the MC's toes. I didn't think they'd take kindly to having part of Alejandro's crew permanently taking up residence here in town.

But I *wanted* to do this. In fact, a part of me *needed* this. I'd had safety after I was rescued because of Walker and his club attachment. How many women were out there that didn't have the same luxury that I was afforded?

Ten minutes later, Walker and Vincent stepped into the room together. Vince had grease on his arms, and there was a smear of it on his cheek. Yet, even though he was dirty and smelled like a grease pit, I still wanted him to fuck me ten ways to Sunday.

Shaking that shit from my head, I grabbed the envelope off the nightstand. "I, um, was left a hefty inheritance," I began, handing the envelope to Walker. He slid the papers out. "That's just my first portion, and there's one million in that account."

Walker and Vincent both watched me, waiting to see where I was going with this. I nervously twisted my fingers in my lap. "I want to open a shelter for women like me," I said softly, my eyes flickering back and forth between the two of them. Nothing showed on their faces. I nervously licked my lips. "I found safety with you two and within this club, but other women might not have something like that and—"

"Breathe," Walker instructed as he took a seat next to me. I sucked in a sharp breath of air. I hadn't even realized I'd been rambling and holding my breath all at once. "Baby, the moment you said you wanted to open a shelter, we were already on board."

My eyes widened in surprise; I turned to look at Vincent. He nodded at me before he gripped the bottom of his shirt and tugged it over his head, dropping it into the hamper near the bathroom door. "We'll take you tomorrow to get you started on licensing," he told me.

I couldn't help the smile that pulled at my lips. Walker's fingers slipped between mine. "That easy?" I asked.

"That easy," Walker assured me.

"There's one more thing, though," I said. They both gave me their undivided attention again, though it was beginning to get hard to concentrate with Vincent standing there with no damn shirt on. "I want the club's protection. These women, they'll need help. They'll be running from abusers, and they'll need to feel safe."

Vincent came over and slanted his lips across mine. I softly moaned into the kiss, my hands coming up to touch his sweaty sides. "Let me shower, and we'll go hunt Copper down to talk to him. Pretty sure he'll agree, though. He's got a soft spot for abused women."

My mind flitted to Penny. Had Penny gone through something horrible, too?

"Okay," I whispered.

Vincent kissed me again before heading into the bathroom, already unfastening his jeans as he went. Walker gripped my chin and turned my head to face him. His lips tenderly brushed mine as he spoke. "I'm proud of you," he said softly.

"For?" I asked, my heart rate quickening at the pride in his voice.

"For doing something that means a lot to you, for wanting to help other women who go through bad shit, too. That takes a special kind of soul to inherit a shit ton of money like that and do something selfless with it, baby girl."

I smiled at him. "You saved me, Walker," I quietly admitted. His eyes softened, and he trailed the tips of his fingers along my jaw. "I want to save people the way you saved me."

He didn't say anything. Instead, he just slanted his lips across mine, his kiss conveying everything he couldn't say with words.

BOOK SEVEN   VINCENT

Copper pulled the chapel door open and beckoned me in before him. Penny followed me in shortly after, and then Vince and Walker walked in. My two men took seats on either side of me, and Penny draped herself across Copper's lap once he was seated.

"Alright, what is it you need to talk to me about?" Copper asked.

I drew in a deep breath and linked my fingers together in my lap. "I want to open a women's shelter in town," I told him.

A sort of respect lit up his eyes. "You need a loan?"

I shook my head. "My parents apparently left me a shit ton of money. I just inherited the first portion of it," I explained. "I just want the club's protection. These women need to feel safe—" I began to explain.

He held up a hand, shutting me up. I swallowed thickly. "Say no more," he told me. My eyes widened in disbelief. Vincent had told me he thought Copper would agree, but I guess a part of me still hadn't been expecting it. "You've got our protection. I'll call up Grim and get him on board as well."

"Grim is the president of the Texas Charter," Penny explained at my confused look.

I pushed my fingers through my hair. "This feels too easy," I confessed. It really did. I'd expected to have to make a business plan, show them I was serious—something.

Penny offered me a soft, understanding smile. "You and I, Nova, are kindred souls. I know the pain you went through." My heart fucking wept for her, cried for the sadness that rang in her eyes. Copper nuzzled her neck, and she drew in a deep breath. "I was lucky to have the Texas Charter before I met Copper."

Right then, I understood why Copper was immediately on board with it. His old lady had gone through her own trauma.

"Thank you," I said softly. Both of my men slid their hands over my thighs, gently squeezing.

"I support family," Copper said, "but even if you weren't family, the moment you said women's shelter, you would have had me on board. You're a special soul," he told me, repeating Walker's words from earlier. "I'm sure once you have the place open, you'll gain a lot of sponsors as well."

Penny cleared her throat. "Count us as sponsors," she told me.

I blinked back tears. "Thank you."

She nodded. Vincent pulled me onto his lap, and Walker grabbed my hands as I burst into tears, overwhelmed with the support I was receiving.

BOOK SEVEN   VINCENT

It all felt too good to be true, but I would take every bit of support being held out to me.

CHAPTER SIXTEEN
VINCENT

I towel-dried my hair, a sliver of water running down my chest. "Surprised Nova isn't up here," I said when Walker stepped into the shower.

"Think she was downstairs helping Penny when we came in earlier," he explained.

That morning, we'd taken her to get started on licensing. It'd been a bit of an exhausting process for her, I could tell, but there wasn't much Walker and I could do about that when we dropped her off because we had to head into work and help play catch up.

There was always so much shit to get done at the garage. It felt never-ending, but that also meant that business was booming for Kyle, and I could never be pissed that a brother was successful.

I tugged on a t-shirt and a pair of jeans before shoving my feet into my boots, heading downstairs to go check on Nova. Her shoulder was still healing, and she didn't need to be using it much. And that wasn't just me being overprotective and worried about her; that was her doctor's orders, too.

I paused when I walked around the bar to where the couches were, a soft smile tilting my lips. She was asleep on the couch, her lips softly parted, light snores escaping her mouth. An open book was resting on her chest, and it looked like Penny had draped a throw blanket over her.

"I didn't want to disturb her," Penny whispered, coming up beside me.

I gently squeezed Penny's shoulder in thanks before moving toward Nova. Penny slipped the book from Nova's hands, and I gently lifted Nova into my arms, throw blanket and all, and carried her up the stairs to put her to bed. Penny set the book on the dresser before slipping out of the room, quietly shutting the door behind her. Walker stepped out of the bathroom, a towel slung low around his waist, his glistening abs on full display for me.

If I didn't have a sleeping woman in my arms, I'd get on my knees and lick all that water from his body. The man was not only a beautiful distraction, but he was also sex-on-a-stick.

I gently laid Nova on the bed while Walker yanked on a pair of sweats. He helped me get her changed into something more comfortable. She moaned in aggravation a couple of times but never fully came awake.

The woman really could sleep like the fucking dead sometimes. It was both worrying and adorable. It made me worry because if something ever happened, her reaction time would be extremely slow. But I guess I should have been happy that she could still sleep so peacefully after all the hell that she had endured.

Walker slid in bed behind her, wrapping her up in his arms as I stripped down to a pair of briefs. Once I was laying in front of her, I maneuvered my arm under her head, a yawn leaving my lips.

"Love you," Walker whispered.

I reached over Nova and laid my hand on his side, my actions saying everything I needed him to know.

Having Nova against my back was . . . blissful. I'd never had a woman on the back of my bike before, and to feel Nova there? It felt *right*.

I slowed to a stop in front of the first place Nova wanted to look at. It was a big ass warehouse for sale for way under the market value. It was slap-dead in the middle of town basically, and the only way to get to the loading docks was through a back alley, which was probably why it hadn't been purchased yet. Most people didn't want to be bothered with those kinds of complications.

Nova slid off my bike and walked over to Walker. He wrapped an arm around her waist and dropped a kiss to her lips. I came up beside her, grabbing her hand in mine. "Want to walk inside?" I asked her, holding the key up. The guy had given it to me. Most people in this town trusted the MC more than the damn cops.

She beamed and nodded her head. I unlocked the steel door and led her inside, flicking on some lights as I went. The space was massive with a good-sized second level. She stepped away from us, walking around the space.

"If she chooses this," Walker said quietly, both of us watching her, "we could easily put walls into the place so everyone has their own rooms. Set up a security room. There's enough space for all of that."

I nodded in agreement. I'd seen the pictures of the other places, but I was hoping she chose this one. It was a damn good price, practically a fucking steal. And it offered way more space than the other places had. Not to mention, it would be a lot easier to put security cameras up with it only having one back entrance—that being the dock—and one front entrance.

"I want this!" she announced from the second floor.

I grinned up at her. "You a hundred percent sure you don't want to look at the other places?"

Smiling, she shook her head. "This place—it feels right."

Walker grinned up at her, his hand finding my back pocket. I jumped when he suddenly squeezed my ass, making Nova giggle. "Well, come on, baby girl. Paperwork doesn't sign itself," he called up to her.

~ * ~ * ~

Five long-ass hours later, Nova had paid cash for the building, paid her closing costs, and was now the proud owner of a warehouse.

Cheers of congratulations met her when we walked into the clubhouse. Penny and Olivia had baked a cake, and the women instantly swept her away from us.

"Well, how's it feel to be with a business owner?" Halen teased. "The sex?"

"Keep on," Walker warned him, bringing the bottle of beer to his lips, "and I'll tell Genesis you're fantasizing about our woman."

Halen scowled. I snorted. Halen may joke around, but we knew Genesis had that man by the balls. He worshipped the ground she walked on.

"Wanted to run something by your girl when she gets a chance," Logan said, walking up to where we were standing.

"Thanks, brother," I said as he handed me a fresh, cold beer. "What do you want to talk to her about?"

Nova walked up to us at that moment. Logan smiled down at her. "Wanted to talk to you," he told her.

Walker grunted since Logan hadn't bothered answering me. Logan just smirked, but still didn't pay us much mind.

"What's that?" Nova asked, forking a piece of cake into her mouth. My jeans tightened at the sight of her wrapping her lips around that fork, and without even glancing at me, she smirked, knowing she had me right where she wanted me.

"It's no secret that all of us have a special interest in what you're trying to do," Logan began. "I don't normally get involved in anything that involves the club when it comes to business, but since you don't wear a cut, and I want to help your cause, I'm putting aside my own feelings. I want to offer security." He caught her plate before she dropped it. "You'd have four men on the clock at all times once you open. I'll put in cameras and my top-of-the-line security system at no charge. Instead of offering money to sponsor you, I'm offering you this."

Walker quickly grabbed her cake plate from her and set it on a table so she wouldn't risk almost dropping it again. I watched as she tried blinking back her tears at his unexpected offer, but two of them escaped, slipping down her pretty face. "You mean that?" she croaked. "I never expected—"

He nodded at her. "I want to help, Nova."

She frantically nodded her head, a disbelieving, watery laugh spilling from her lips. "I'd love to have it," she told him. Surprising him, she threw her arms around his neck. He quickly hugged her in return before releasing her so she could quickly step back. She swiped at her cheeks just as Kyle came up. I bit back a smile because I knew our woman was going to end up in tears before all of this was over, but they would be the good tears, the only kind of tears I ever wanted her to shed.

Because when she was happy, she cried so fucking prettily.

"I want to offer sponsorship as well," Kyle told her. "You have the full backing of Frazier's."

Nova sobbed.

Genesis strode up with her hand in Halen's. "Halen and I will be supporting as well," she told Nova. "We don't have a business, but we do have quite a bit of money."

Walker wrapped his arms around our woman, helping to keep her on her feet. I just stood back and watched as our family stepped forward, each man individually offering sponsorship that was separate from the club's.

Nova had done something amazing by opening this shelter. Too many women were victims of men and the pain they were capable of inflicting.

This entire club would stand behind her—always. And every member of this club would stand behind her cause.

CHAPTER SEVENTEEN
WALKER

I never believed that happiness like this was attainable for a man like me.

I was dark. I was fucked up. My demons clouded most of my days.

But with one fucking smile from Nova, the demons inside of me just went . . . silent.

Like a goddamn miracle had happened.

I hadn't had a depressive episode in fucking weeks. I was sleeping better, my flashbacks rarely plaguing my dreams anymore. Even my fucking moods were better, and the entire club was noticing it.

The few times I'd been dragged down by a flashback, Nova had woken up with me every time, and she wrapped herself around my body like a monkey, her fingers running through my hair. And then Vince would wrap himself around me from behind, both of them working to make me feel safe again.

I had never realized how much I needed someone like Nova until I had her. She evened out Vincent's rough edges. He was still my rock, but Nova was the buoy that kept my head above the fucking water.

I felt like I could fucking *breathe* again.

And this feeling—I never wanted to let go of it.

Hence why I was now hunting down Vincent to talk to him about one of us marrying Nova.

Vince looked up as I stepped into the backyard. We bought this house with cash a couple of weeks ago. Vince and I never thought we'd see the day that we were willingly moving out of the clubhouse, but here we were, living on fucking thirty-three acres of land in a ranch-style home.

All for Nova so she could have a home outside of the clubhouse.

Shit still blew my mind sometimes.

Guess this was the kind of shit that happened when you settled down and found yourself an old lady.

"Hey, babe," he greeted. Not giving a shit about the grease on his hands or smeared on his cheek, I gripped the side of his neck and slanted my lips across his. He moaned softly, his hands grasping my hips, yanking me closer to him. Once we parted, he licked his lips, his eyes darkening. "Hell of a greeting."

I grinned. "Missed you, but need to talk about something."

He snorted. "Babe, I've been back here all goddamn day working on this piece of shit."

I glanced at the old Ford truck he was restoring. Vince was a fanatic for car restorations. He always bought them, restored them, and if he didn't want to keep the vehicle once it was done, he sold it for a fucking fine-ass dollar.

"I think one of us should propose to Nova," I told him.

He walked over to the sink he'd installed outside and began scrubbing his hands. "Needs to be you," he told me.

His answer surprised me. "Me?" I asked.

He nodded, his back still to me as he scrubbed at a grease spot on his arm. "Yeah, babe—you. No offense to our woman, but if I marry anyone, I'd marry you." A soft smile tilted my lips at his confession. "So, you marry her."

"You sure about this, Vince?" I asked him.

He turned to face me, drying his hands on a clean hand towel. "More than sure. You fell in love with her first. She's the reason you kept pushing so hard to come back home to me. You have a different bond with her than I do," I frowned; he stepped forward, "but I'm *okay* with that, Walker. You and I have a bond that's different than what she shares with you. The three of us fit together so fucking well because the three of us each bring something different to the table." A crooked smile lifted his lips. "I love you, and I want you to marry her."

Unable to help myself, I grabbed him and kissed him again. Vincent groaned and backed me up against the truck. I jumped onto the tailgate and yanked him between my thighs, our tongues lashing together, our hands tearing at our clothes.

Nova was at the clubhouse, prepping food with the other club women, which left me and Vince together by ourselves. And while I loved having our woman with us, sometimes I needed this with Vince—just this one-on-one time.

"Fuck—lube," Vince hissed.

"Grab something from the kitchen," I told him.

He pressed a hard kiss to my lips before rushing inside, his hard dick bouncing against his stomach as he rushed away from me, slipping inside for a moment. He came out a few seconds later with the olive oil. I snickered.

"Nova will kill us."

He shrugged, pouring some onto his hand. "I'll replace it."

He hooked his elbows beneath the back of my knees and spread me wide before sinking inside of me. I moaned, my back arching. Reaching for him, I grabbed the back of his neck and pulled him down to me. He pumped in and out of me as our mouths worked together, our kiss sloppy and heated, but God, it felt so fucking amazing.

"No matter what you share with her or what I share with her," Vincent panted, "we will still always belong to each other."

I nodded in agreement and sealed our lips together again, my muscles already tightening, ready to fall off that edge with him. Vince grabbed my shaft in his oily hands and pumped me once, twice, three times, and together, we soared off the fucking edge.

Vincent nodded once at me from across the room. The club knew about us by now, and honestly, it didn't make my skin crawl. No one had made a big deal about it either. They'd just gone on about their day.

I think most of them had suspected it.

I love you, he mouthed.

Nodding once, I drew in a deep breath and then cleared my throat, moving towards Nova who was laughing with the other club women, the kids playing on the floor around them. I ruffled Randall's hair as I passed him before dropping to one knee in front of Nova.

Her squeal silenced the entire clubhouse. I flipped open the ring box.

"Yes!" she screamed.

I laughed, hanging my head, shaking it. *This woman, I swear.* I looked back up at her. "Woman, I didn't even ask the question."

"Yes, I want to marry you!" she told me. "You don't even have to ask."

With that, she launched herself at me, and I barely refrained from crashing onto my back. I caught her in my arms, and she pressed her lips to mine, giving me a kiss that was *definitely* too heated for any child to witness.

When she pulled back, she took the ring box out of my hand and slipped the ring on her finger. I glanced behind me at Vincent. His shoulders were shaking with laughter.

Our woman was definitely one of a kind.

I looked back at Nova as congratulations sounded around us. "I love you," I told her.

Her fucking beaming smile was all the reply I needed from her before she kissed me again.

CHAPTER EIGHTEEN
NOVA

I blew out a soft breath, checking myself in the reflection one more time. Today was the opening day for my shelter—Nova's Sanctuary—and to say that I was nervous about it was a fucking understatement.

The amount of support I'd received from numerous businesses in town had blown my mind. I'd never expected my nonprofit to blow up as it had.

"You ready, baby girl?" Vince softly asked me from the doorway to my office. "Everyone is waiting on you."

I nodded and turned to face him. He grinned. "You look fucking amazing, and if you didn't need to be downstairs to greet everyone, I'd bend you over your fucking desk."

My nipples pebbled beneath the dress I was wearing. It was a black lace dress that stopped at mid-thigh, and I was wearing a pair of silver heels with it, my hair curled around my shoulders.

Breathing out a soft laugh, he held his hand out to me, and without hesitation, I grabbed it, allowing him to lead me from my office. Walker met us at the top of the stairs, and he grabbed my other hand, both of my men flanking me as we reached the bottom.

Cheers of congratulations met my ears. So many people had shown up today to help me celebrate—at least one person and their plus ones from each business that was supporting this cause, every single member of the SCMC, both mother charter and Texas charter, Alejandro and some of his men, the Sons of Hell, and the Texas charter of Satan's Worshippers.

All of the support was a bit overwhelming, but I was definitely happy to have it.

Within the first hour, I'd already greeted so many people that it was beginning to do my head in. My cheeks were beginning to hurt from smiling so much, but the entire ordeal was made easier by either Vincent's or Walker's firm, reassuring touches at my back. They always alternated, but I was never left alone at any time.

Finally, I got a little reprieve after we cut the cake. Vincent fed me a slice, groaning when I wrapped my lips around the fork.

"I can imagine those pretty lips wrapped around something else, too," Walker breathed in my ear. Tingles rushed down my spine.

"Speaking of sex," I said, glancing between the two of them, a smirk curving my lips. I rested my hand on my belly. "We have a little surprise due in a little less than eight months."

It took a moment for them to realize what I was getting at, but then their eyes widened at the same time. "You're pregnant?!" Vincent exclaimed, making the room go quiet.

My cheeks flamed with heat as I nodded. Another round of congratulations went up, but after my announcement, Walker and Vince didn't let many people close to me for fear something would happen.

And honestly, I reveled in their overprotectiveness. Most women might have become agitated, but with the hell I'd gone through, I loved my men being extra careful with me.

I'd come out of hell a shell of myself, but I'd been determined to live, to continue surviving. Walker had given me a purpose, but the two of my men together? I had thrived.

My throat burned with sudden tears. "Thank you," I told them both, my voice hoarse.

Walker's brows furrowed. "What for, baby girl?"

I sniffled, a tear running down my cheek. "For loving me," I whispered. "I couldn't—wouldn't—have accomplished any of this without the two of you at my sides."

Vincent gripped my chin and turned my head to face him. His lips brushed over mine. "Nothing to thank us for, sweet girl. You're our beginning and our end." He brushed his nose with mine. "Now, enjoy your success. I know there's a hell of a lot more where this came from."

I swiped at my cheeks, smiling at them both. Walker wrapped his arms around me from behind, resting his chin on the top of my head, and Vincent grabbed my hand in his, lacing our fingers together.

This.

This right here—this was paradise.

I was home.

NEW MC SERIES SNEAK PEEK
BLOODY ROYALS

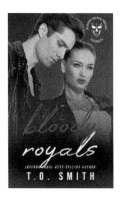

Link to Order Book One:
https://books2read.com/bloodyroyals

Katie

Darkness.

It was the first thing I noticed when I ripped my eyes open, leaving me to wonder for a moment if my eyes had ever really been closed in the first place.

I sat stock-still, taking in what I could through my other senses. My legs and arms were tied to a chair—a hard one at that, considering my ass was sore. I wiggled a little, taking note that whoever had tied me to this chair had done a damn good job. I had almost no wiggle room.

There was a gag in my mouth, which didn't surprise me. It was rough, but the material was thin. Pretty sure it was a bandana.

I didn't know how I ended up here, so chances were, I'd done my classic Katie thing and ran my mouth.

Dad had always warned me that my mouth would one day land me in trouble he couldn't save me from. I'd just never truly believed him because Dad was *always* there.

Drawing in a deep breath through my nose, I closed my eyes, trying to think of the last thing I *could* remember.

Zachary Taylor.

That name alone sent chills down my spine as well as made me feel sick to my stomach.

I blocked that shit from my mind, deciding not to focus on that. If that was the last thing I remembered, then I had either been kidnapped not too long after that incident, or I'd been hit so hard I lost some of my memory.

But my head didn't hurt, which kind of ruled out the last option.

My stomach rumbled; I rolled my eyes. Of course, I was fucking hungry. It seemed no matter how shitty of a situation I got in, I could always seem to be hungry.

It was a curse, really.

VINCENT

The creaking of a door reached my ears before I heard it click shut a moment later. I held my breath for a moment, trying to make out some other sound. No other sound came.

But a fucking light flickered on overhead.

My curse was muffled by my gag as I squinted, trying to give my eyes time to adjust. I quickly took in what I could. The walls were concrete and bare. There were some pipes running along the wall, and there was a set of stairs off to my right.

The basement seemed to be neglected—never used—apart from me now being in it.

Voices flooded into the room at the same time that feet pounded down the stairs, bringing the once oppressing room to life. Three guys came around the wall, all of them built, their faces expressionless, all of them staring at me.

Fear sliced through my veins. I locked it away, channeling it as I had been raised to do since I was a small child. It was a survival mechanism that had been ingrained in me from the moment I was old enough to understand the kind of life I had been born into.

It wasn't for the weak of heart or the weak of mind.

I quickly took in the three men in front of me, engraining them into my head with a vivid picture. One of the guys was olive-skinned, his hair cut into a buzz cut, tattoos swirling over his scalp. He was muscular—beefy, like he worked out a lot in his spare time. His eyes were a deep, dark chocolate color, but they were cold, void of any real emotion.

One of the other guys had longer, brown hair that slightly hung into his blue eyes. He wasn't as muscular as the olive-skinned guy, but the look he gave everything around him sent chills down my spine. He was dangerous—that much was clear.

The other guy really caught my attention, and I hated that I found him extremely attractive.

Dirty blonde hair and dark eyes sucked me in, holding me captive in his gaze. His jawline was a strong, sharp line that made him look absolutely perfect. His cheekbones were high on his face, giving him a very slim appearance that matched the rest of his body.

He was tall with a lankier build, but when he moved, his muscles flexed, letting me know that just because he was smaller than the other two, he held his own power, which was even more dangerous.

The man I had been admiring stepped up so that he was right in front of me. I quickly looked down, showing submission. I had to play this smart. I knew I could handle my own, but not while I was tied to a chair. Right now, I was at a disadvantage.

Right then, submission would get me a hell of a lot further than bravery ever would.

"Look at me," he finally commanded. His voice was rough and slightly gravelly and extremely deep, which I hadn't been expecting from him.

That voice held no room for argument or non-compliance. I surprised myself when I obediently snapped my head up to look at him. My breath caught in my throat. Up close, this man was absolutely breathtaking, a beauty that was both deadly and cruel.

He suddenly cursed, making me flinch back from him, and he spun around to face the other two guys. His jaw was ticking furiously, his hands clenched into fists at his sides. "Who the fuck is this?!" he roared, slinging his arm back towards me, almost hitting me in the face, but somehow stopping his hand just short of doing so.

"This is the girl you asked for," the olive-skinned guy responded, frowning at the man in front of me.

"You two are fucking idiots," he snarled. "Shut it!" he yelled when the brunette guy opened his mouth to speak. "This isn't the fucking girl I asked for. I gave you two idiots a fucking *picture*, and you *still* couldn't do the goddamn job correctly." He breathed out heavily and unclenched his fists, then clenched them again. I swallowed thickly, watching as the veins in his arms stood out against his skin. He roughly pointed to the door.

"Get the fuck out of my sight," he snarled.

They walked out of the room, leaving me alone with the monster in charge of this entire thing. He turned to me and glared, a sneer twisting his lips. "You'll just stay down here until I can figure out what the fuck to do with you," he spat, turning on his heel without another word, leaving me gagged and tied to the chair.

He stormed up the stairs, his boots pounding against the steps. The light eventually turned off, and I heard the door slam closed right after. I clenched my jaw, fisting my hands behind me.

When I got out of this place and back home, these mother fuckers would pay for crossing me.

I'd make damn sure of it.

The light turned on in the room again before the door even completely opened up. I strained my ears, listening as a set of boots began pounding down the stairs. My heart began to race. These steps were drunk and sloppy, a sound I was extremely familiar with. I'd fought off so many drunken assholes that I'd lost count, but now, I was bound and gagged.

I had no way to fight off this man's advances.

The man stepped down into the room, stopping in front of me. He was shorter than the three men that had been in here earlier, but he was well built—more so than the olive-skinned guy. And looking into his eyes, I instantly knew he was drunk. They weren't focusing all that well, his eyes way too dilated, and they were beyond bloodshot.

My heart raced in my chest, and I felt sick to my stomach. I'd been around enough drunk men to know what could happen to me if I didn't somehow get loose. This man could very well do whatever he wanted to me, and no one would hear me screaming.

"You're a pretty little thing," he slurred, his words almost incoherent. I tilted my chin up in bravery despite me feeling anything but brave at that moment. *Channel your fear, Katie.* "Heard you got mixed up in this bullshit." He laughed. "Travis said you ain't good for much else besides some pussy if we keep you around." He leaned in close to me. I gagged at the smell of his breath which was a horrible mix of beer, weed, pussy, and seafood. "Thought I'd come down and get myself a little taste, sweetheart," he leered, running his eyes over my body.

I was still in the clothes from my date, my top showing a lot of cleavage, my shorts so tight it was a shock they didn't cut my circulation off. My black combat boots were on my feet, but sometime while I'd been unconscious, my leather jacket had gone missing.

I hated that he was able to see every part of me so easily, even with clothes on.

I glared at him, biting back tears as he grabbed the neckline of my tank top, ripping it off of me so roughly, my chair toppled to the floor. I bit back a yelp of pain as I landed painfully on my arm.

My bra was the next thing to go, and he tossed it somewhere across the room. After righting my chair back up, his grubby hands reached out, and he roughly cupped my breasts, pinching and rolling my nipples to the point pain raced through my chest.

"Fucking amazing tits," he drunkenly slurred, leaning forward, biting at my skin. I tightened my hands, wishing I were free so I could bash his fucking skull into my knee before I slit his throat with something.

A rough cry of pain ripped from my throat, muffled by the gag, as he roughly bit my nipple. "You like that, don't you? Dirty bitches like you always enjoy pain," he rambled.

I glared at him, my chest heaving. I had to get loose.

My hands were itching to break his fucking neck.

He pulled a knife out of his pocket. A plan quickly formed in my mind. If I could get somewhat loose, I could gain the upper hand.

Using the knife, he cut my leg restraints, which was his first mistake. As soon as my legs were loose, I kicked him in the face, sending my chair flying backward with the force I put behind it. He sprawled backward across the floor, roaring out in pain, blood spurting from his nose. I crashed roughly down on my arms.

He yanked me off the chair and threw me onto the floor, my arms still bound behind my back. My head roughly slammed against the cement floor beneath me, and black spots danced in my vision. I rapidly blinked, trying to fight past the darkness threatening to swarm my vision.

He climbed on top of me, and before I could kick him again, he sat on top of my legs, pinning me down as he turned his body to yank my boots off my feet. I bucked my hips beneath him, trying to get him off of me, but he was too heavy. The only thing moving beneath him seemed to do was make him harder.

Disgust crawled up my veins.

He yanked my shorts apart with sheer, drunken strength, and ripped my underwear off. I fought harder, but I was fucked—royally fucked. I wasn't getting out of this situation. There was no fucking hope for me. Even when he slid off my legs, he just held them down with his hands so I couldn't move them.

I glared up at the ceiling, gritting my teeth, so much rage pulsing through me that it made it hard to fucking think.

I was going to be raped.

Right as he was about to push into me, someone yanked him off of me. I heard a fist hit skin, but I didn't turn to look. I curled into a ball, trying to hide the most important parts of my body.

The olive-skinned guy from earlier dragged a now dead, bloody man towards the other side of the room. The ringleader knelt in front of me a moment later, his dark eyes intent on my face. I tilted my chin up at him, refusing to be worn down.

A small smile tilted his lips.

"I'm not going to hurt you," he said softly. I wanted to scoff. I was kidnapped, and he wanted me to trust him when he said he wasn't going to hurt me? "You're safe with me." He slowly extended his hand out to me. I just gritted my teeth, staring between his face and his hand. When he saw I wasn't going to freak out, he reached forward with his other hand to untie the gag.

I worked my jaw around, loving the freedom I had to move it now. Soreness rang through my jaw, but I pushed it down. Pain was weakness, and I would not be weak in this situation.

I went back to watching him. I didn't trust this man at all. I saw how he had acted earlier, and I didn't need him lashing out at me unexpectedly. Right now, I still knew that submission was going to be more useful than my bravery.

"My name is Travis," he told me. "What's yours?"

I continued watching him for another moment before I answered. "Katie," I finally replied.

He nodded, acknowledging my name. "I'm going to untie your wrists and take you upstairs. You can get a shower, and I'll have Grace make you something to eat."

I didn't say anything - just nodded my head at him. He untied my wrists, then proceeded to take his shirt off. I barely kept myself from licking my lips at the sight of all those muscles and tattoos on display. Sure, he had a lanky build, but there wasn't an ounce of fat on him. His upper body flexed with every move he made to pull his shirt over his head.

And he had a damn V that was sure to drive me fucking wild.

He handed me his shirt with a smirk when he caught me running my eyes over him. I just evenly met his gaze as I took his shirt from him and slipped it over my head, almost moaning at the smell of it. It smelled like a very expensive cologne mixed with the smell of pure man.

It was almost orgasm-inducing.

He held his hand out to me when I got ready to push myself off the floor, but I ignored it, standing up on my own. His shirt was enough help. Everything came with a price. Even normal, small shit that a normal person wouldn't think twice about, there was always some kind of price tag involved in it.

Where I came from, you didn't take help unless you absolutely needed it. Because when it came time to pay back your debt, you had better be fucking ready.

He eyed me for a moment like he was trying to figure something out. When I arched a single eyebrow at him, he just turned on his heel and started walking toward the stairs. I followed him out of the basement into a hallway. Exquisite paintings hung on the walls, and a soft, burgundy carpet covered the floor.

Whoever Travis was, he was obviously wealthy.

And money made men like him even deadlier. Because with money, came power.

We walked up a spiral staircase and down another hall until he led me into a bedroom that smelled exactly like his shirt.

I quickly took in my surroundings, committing it all to memory—my survival mechanism.

The bedsheets on the bed were black, along with the comforter. It was a huge California King bed that looked extremely comfortable. The bed frame was brown along with the rest of his furniture. He definitely knew how to color code, which strangely pleased me. Things not matching really fucked with me, even if it wasn't my own space to have any say-so.

"There should be some clothes in the bottom drawer of the dresser," he said, pointing at one of the dressers near the closet, "that I think will fit you. Lock the bathroom and bedroom door so no one else will try any stupid shit. But because this is my room and my bathroom, I have a key to get in and out," he warned me.

I nodded in reply. He walked out of the room without another word or glance, shutting the door behind him. I did as he said and locked the bedroom door behind him. Then, I went into the bathroom and shut and locked that door behind me so I could hopefully take a shower in peace.

I sighed in contentment when I took in the bathroom. It was spacious with a marble sink and a huge hot tub. His shower had multiple shower heads that came from practically all directions. I was already in love with his shower.

The man knew how to live in style.

Though I wanted to enjoy the shower, I knew I was in enemy territory, so I hurriedly did what I needed, keeping my ears peeled for any kind of noise that would signal someone else in the bedroom or the bathroom.

When I stepped out, I wrapped a towel around me. Turning around, I was surprised to find Travis leaning against the doorjamb of the bathroom, a small smirk tilting his lips, his dark eyes running sensually over my body.

How the fuck had I not heard him?

I picked up the nearest thing to me, but he arched an eyebrow at me, standing up straighter and taking a step into the bathroom. "I wouldn't do that if I were you," he warned me. "I'm being a decent guy by taking you out of the basement and letting you shower, put on clean clothes, and eat. But test me, Katie, and I'll lock you back down there."

I gritted my teeth, glaring at him as I slowly set down the hairbrush I'd been holding. His smirk widened. "You're hot as fuck, Katie," he told me softly, his words twisting around my body like a caress.

I rolled my eyes at him, doing my best to appear unaffected all while my pussy clenched. This was wrong—

wrong on so many fucking levels. I could *not* be turned on by the man who was fucking holding me as a prisoner.

He set a toothbrush on the bathroom counter. "Thought you might need this," he said in way of explanation.

I nodded at him in thanks. His eyes slowly trailed over me one more time, and then, he smirked again before stepping out of the bathroom.

To say that his heated gaze hadn't left me breathless would be a lie. That man's gaze was so heated when he was looking at me, I almost broke out in a sweat. Every part of my body was tingling, desperately wanting him to touch me.

Get a fucking grip, I chastised myself.

Once I was dressed, I brushed my teeth and used the hairbrush on the counter to brush my hair. After, I walked out into the hall, my stomach rumbling. Travis had said he was going to feed me, so there couldn't be any harm in me going to find the kitchen, right?

I stopped at the bottom of the stairs, the sound of Travis speaking reaching my ears. Staying as quiet as I possibly could, I strained my ears to listen to what was being said.

"We can't just fucking *let her go*. You two fucked up—as usual—and now I have to figure out a way to clean up your fucking mess," I heard Travis say. He abruptly stopped, clearing his throat. "You can come out, Katie."

Fuck.

Did anything slip past this man?

I stepped off the bottom step, coming around the wall to face Travis. His eyes held annoyance, but he didn't say anything. He just crooked a finger at me and turned on his heel, a silent order for me to follow him.

The olive-skinned guy didn't even spare me a glance as he turned away and moved further down the hall in the opposite direction we were going.

When I stepped into the kitchen behind Travis, I instantly spotted a woman at the stove. Her back was turned to me. She had graying hair, and she was a bit shorter than I was.

She turned to face us when we entered the kitchen. She looked to be in her late fifties, possibly early sixties. She had blue eyes that were full of a lot more life than anyone else's around here that I had come across so far.

She moved around the island in the center of the kitchen and wrapped Travis up in a hug. Surprising me, he hugged her back, pressing a kiss to the top of her head before stepping back from her. "I didn't know you were back home, boy. Did they get that girl you were looking for?"

And I was supposed to trust this bitch to cook my fucking food?

Travis clenched his jaw. He was obviously still pissed off about the guys' mistake. "No; instead, they got this girl, "he said, waving his hand in my direction. The gray-haired woman looked over at me, a frown pulling at her lips. "She doesn't even look like her." Travis shook his head. "I'm working on cleaning the situation up."

I narrowed my eyes at him. What the fuck was that supposed to mean?

The woman shook her head. She then turned to me. "Are you hungry, dear?"

I just stared at her, biting my tongue so I wouldn't lash out at both of them. Travis glared at me. "She asked you a fucking question," he snapped.

God, grant me strength—and not physical.

I glared back at him before turning my attention to the woman that had been cooking. "Yeah," I grumbled. I really didn't trust her to cook my food, but I didn't trust anyone else here, either. So, I would just have to eat and hope for the fucking best. Always knew my time on Earth was limited anyway with me being the Bloody Royals MC's president's daughter.

"Watch over her while I get some shit straightened out," Travis told her.

He walked out of the room without waiting for an answer.

Dick.

She went to the stove to cook me something to eat, and I sat on a stool at the marble bar. Everything in the kitchen was spotless. How in the hell did you keep a kitchen spotless? The kitchen back at the clubhouse looked like a war zone ninety-nine percent of the time.

"Are you the only woman here?" I asked her.

She shook her head. "No. There are other women here. They keep the boys happy."

So, I'm guessing they're the equivalents of club whores.

"Were they kidnapped, too?" I bluntly asked her.

She looked at me over her shoulder. "No, dear. You're the only person they've kidnapped, and it wasn't even supposed to be you, but I'm sure you already know that." She obviously liked to talk. "The girl that was supposed to be kidnapped is in an abusive situation, and she contacted Travis a couple of weeks ago for help. Travis made plans to help her out of it, but Luke and Ryan screwed it up." She sighed. "And now, they're going to catch heat for you being kidnapped instead."

He had no fucking clue who I was. None of them did.

I smirked. Being the Bloody Royals MC's princess might finally have another perk.

"Maybe you should have Travis do a background check on me," I told her. "Trust me, my people aren't going to call the cops to get help. They'll come find me themselves, and when they do, you'd better pray for everyone involved." Her face paled a tiny bit at my words. "Anyone involved in my kidnapping will *not* make it out alive," I warned her.

My dad, James Holland, was an outlaw legend, as was the Bloody Royals MC. They had murdered more people than I could count. My dad had his fingers dug in pies all around the country with connections that ran so deep, none of his members ever served real time for their crimes.

James Holland was a ruthless son of a bitch, and he wasn't afraid to drop bodies.

She set a plate in front of me with a grilled ham and cheese sandwich. "Your people?" she asked. "What do you mean by *your people*?"

I took a bite out of the sandwich. Cheesy goodness exploded in my mouth, and I took a moment to savor it before I answered her. "My dad's the president of the Bloody Royals MC," I told her, dropping the bomb without care.

The blood drained out of her face, making her go as pale as a ghost. "You're kidding, right?" she asked me, desperation filling her voice.

I shook my head at her. "I don't joke about my family." I really didn't. Family was the most important thing to anyone involved in the club. At the end of the day, if you didn't have anything else, you had the Bloody Royals. We were a family, and though I wasn't a guy, I was a part of their brotherhood. They welcomed me in like one of their own.

Travis came into the kitchen at that moment, his eyes landing on Grace's pale face almost immediately. "Everything alright, Grace?" he asked her.

My lips twitched with a smirk.

Katie: 1. Travis: 0.

Her eyes met his, fear lurking in their blue depths. "Travis, I think Luke and Ryan may have made the biggest mistake of their lives—of *all* of our lives."

His eyebrows pulled together, confusion evident on his features. "It's nothing that can't be fixed." I *almost* snorted. "Grace, what's wrong?"

She ran her hands down her aging face, clearly distressed by what I had told her. She waved her hand in my direction—almost helplessly. "Travis, meet Katie Holland, the daughter of the president of the Bloody Royals."

Travis didn't even look at me. He stormed out of the room, and a moment later, I heard him shouting at someone. I finished eating my food, feeling a bit better now that I wasn't walking on eggshells any longer.

I had nothing to be worried about now.

No one wanted to fuck with the Bloody Royals. And if you screwed with me, you screwed with the entire club.

I walked into what I guessed to be the living room after I finished eating. The olive-skinned guy was sprawled out on the floor, blood running down his face, his eyes swollen and bruising. "Damn you, Ryan!" Travis hollered.

"Bashing his face in won't solve anything," I said to Travis as I leaned against the doorjamb of the living room, crossing my arms over my chest.

Travis stormed over to me, grabbing my arm in a grip so tight I knew it would leave bruises. He yanked me close to him, sending me crashing against his body. I immediately recoiled at the murderous gleam in his eyes. I'd been faced with some terrifying men in my life, but none of them had the look in their eyes that Travis now held in his.

"I'd advise you to watch where the fuck you're stepping," Travis sneered. "I'm a hairsbreadth away from snapping your thin, little neck." He tightened his grip. I kept my face schooled, not showing my pain. "Unlike everyone else here, I'm not afraid of James fucking Holland, so get off that fucking pedestal while you can, Katie Holland, before I knock your fucking ass off of it. *I run shit around here, and it'll do you fucking good to remember that.*"

With that, he shoved me against the wall and stormed out of the room. I gritted my teeth, glaring after him until he disappeared from my sight. Ryan got off the floor, his bruised, swollen eyes meeting mine.

"Trust me, I'd listen to him," he warned me. "Travis is a lot more dangerous than your dad." I scoffed. "Travis has zero-tolerance for bikers. This isn't fucking child's play, Katie. Travis is not one to fuck with." He shook his head, wincing. "I don't think your dad is willing to cross Travis, not even for his own daughter. It'd be in your best interest to resume back to the way you were, or you'll find that your dad is just a mere princess compared to that man."

"Travis is a fucking pussy," I spat at him.

Ryan smirked at me, even though his jaw was swelling and his lip was busted. "I'm just giving you a fair warning, princess." I glared at him for the name. "You don't want to cross Travis. You just made your life ten times worse by announcing that you're Katie Holland. The rest of us may be afraid of you because of who you're tied to, but Travis hates your dad and every other biker known to man, which includes *you*. You cross him enough, Holland, and he'll have your blood on his hands."

With that, he walked out of the room. I slumped against the wall as soon as I was alone, my heart thumping hard against my breastbone. I swallowed thickly.

I had a feeling that what Ryan said was true, that I had just dug myself into an even deeper hole.

Dad always said I had a habit of doing that.

And this time, I might have to learn how to survive by myself.

Because Dad wasn't here to save me this time.

PLEASE LEAVE A REVIEW!

I would love to hear what you thought about the book!

Please hop over to Amazon, Goodreads, and/or BookBub and drop your review!

Every review, even the bad ones, is greatly appreciated!

Amazon: https://mybook.to/vincent-tosmith

BookBub: https://www.bookbub.com/books/vincent-savage-crows-mc-mother-charter-book-7-by-t-o-smith

Goodreads: https://www.goodreads.com/book/show/60483815-

OTHER BOOKS BY T.O. SMITH

Find them on Amazon:

https://www.amazon.com/author/tosmith

Find them on her website:

https://tosmithbooks.com

FOLLOW T.O. SMITH

Facebook: https://www.facebook.com/authortosmith

Facebook group: https://www.facebook.com/groups/TOSmith

Instagram: https://www.instagram.com/authortosmith

Patreon: https://www.patreon.com/tiffwritesromance

Twitter: https://www.twitter.com/tiffwritesbooks

TikTok: https://www.tiktok.com/@tiffwritesromance

ABOUT THE AUTHOR

T.O. Smith believes in one thing – a happily ever after.

Her books are fast-paced and dive straight into the romance and the action. She doesn't do extensively drawn-out plots. Normally, within the first chapter, she's got you - hook, line, and sinker.

As a writer of various different genres of romance, a reader is almost guaranteed to find some kind of romance novel they'll enjoy on her page.

T.O. Smith can be found on Facebook, Instagram, Twitter, and now even TikTok! She loves interacting with all of her readers, so follow her!

Printed in Poland
by Amazon Fulfillment
Poland Sp. z o.o., Wrocław

25430376R00079